Bong Trees in Bellingham

A Novel

Christopher Malone
www.bongtreesinbellingham.com

iUniverse, Inc.
New York   Bloomington

Bong Trees in Bellingham
A Novel

This is a work of fiction. All of the characters, names, incidents, organizations, and dialogue in this novel are either the products of the author's imagination or are used fictitiously.

iUniverse books may be ordered through booksellers or by contacting:

iUniverse
1663 Liberty Drive
Bloomington, IN 47403
www.iuniverse.com
1-800-Authors (1-800-288-4677)

Because of the dynamic nature of the Internet, any Web addresses or links contained in this book may have changed since publication and may no longer be valid. The views expressed in this work are solely those of the author and do not necessarily reflect the views of the publisher, and the publisher hereby disclaims any responsibility for them.

ISBN: 978-1-4401-7045-4 (pbk)
ISBN: 978-1-4401-7046-1 (ebk)

Printed in the United States of America

iUniverse rev. date: 06/30/2011

Dedication

This book is dedicated to all victims of injustice, wherever in the world, with a prayer for their comfort, their vindication and their retribution.

And to all who are in love.

And to James and Francis.

Acknowledgements

I ACKNOWLEDGE THE UNWITTING CONTRIBUTIONS of two authors, whose real-life experiences and research provided invaluable information and inspiration to the writing of my book:

Ms. Kathryn Lyon, whose non-fiction book *Witch Hunt,* supported by painstaking research, chronicles a series of injustices in the State of Washington that arose from the so-called "child hearsay laws."

Mr. Donn Fendler, whose childhood adventure and near-tragedy, is told in his book *Lost on a Mountain in Maine.*

And I thank the many people of Whatcom County, not only in Bellingham, but also in Maple Falls and Glacier, who helped me in putting together background material for the book. Any inaccuracies are the result of my not paying attention to what they told me, or of my indulging in literary license to make the story move along.

While the central event of the novel was inspired by documented abuses by the State of Washington and local investigators and prosecutors, the story is pure fiction. Every novel must have a venue, and I have chosen Whatcom County, because that is where Mt. Baker is. Persons and agencies in the novel should not be identified with actual persons or agencies in Whatcom County.

CHAPTER ONE

"LITTLE GIRL, YOU ARE TOAST!" Miss Sarah Noll heard these words directed at her from a passerby, as she walked through the hallway, following the signs to the auditorium. Today, Sarah was representing Point Loma High School in the California High School Individual Cross-Examination Debate finals, held at Stanford University. Her opponent was Theodore Hall III, who was the reigning champion, representing Stanford University High School.

For the last two years, the Stanford Standard had cheered him as "Ted the Terminator" as he trounced one opponent after another. He was famous for unsettling opponents, often to the point of tears. Sarah had seen in the semifinals what he did to a Vietnamese-American girl, who clearly had a superior argument, but whose language skills could not match Hall's quick returns of smooth wit and derision. She had left the podium in tears, as her immigrant parents looked on.

Hall hadn't seen a red-haired girl in the audience fix him with a stare, her face set with firm resolve.

Sarah's debate coach had told her, "He's articulate and arrogant, and short on substance. Do your homework. Attack his factual errors. Go on the offense. And don't let him rattle you."

Today, Sarah was dressed in a navy blue skirt, a white blouse, and a floppy dark blue tie. Her red hair stood out in shocks on either side, before falling down. She was facing a hostile, hometown audience. She was cool and composed.

Sarah had always prided herself on her lucid presentations of facts

1

supporting her cogent arguments, delivered in a polite, organized and faultless manner. Her vanquished opponents were her biggest admirers.

But today, it was time to take off the gloves. He won't make *me* cry, Sarah determined; I'm going to make *him* cry.

The judges were a panel of academics headed by the Chancellor of the University of California. The annual Individual Cross-Examination Debate championship was an important event.

Hall had a large cheering section filling most of the front rows. Sarah's supporters were only an ample Russian woman in a simple print dress, flanked by a tall, thin boy, and a strikingly pretty Asian girl.

The moderator introduced both contestants. The topic of debate was: "Resolved, that the United States should use its economic and moral power to curtail child labor abuses worldwide."

Hall's opening statement: "The US is not the world's policeman. We don't have the right to dictate to the rest of the world, their internal labor policies. These economies aren't like ours. Often, the income that a child produces is necessary to the survival of the family.

The US economy is benefited by these low labor costs. We purchase things that are imported, cheaply. This means that we have more money left over to buy other things that may be made by American labor, or local services. Everyone is better off.

We are part of a global economy, and we'd better get used to the idea. Free trade benefits all. The United States is a member of the World Trade Organization, and as we benefit from the rules, we are likewise obligated to follow the rules in our dealings with our trade partners."

Noll's opening statement: "The United States is a sovereign nation. We have the right to determine the terms under which we trade and invest. We should not force other countries to bend to our will, but we do have the right, as has any nation, to control our trade and investment.

And when we see these abuses against children in country after country, we have the right and the moral obligation to withhold our purchasing and investment power in order to guide these countries into morally acceptable behavior."

Hall: "The World Trade Organization, the WTO, has created a framework for cooperation among all the member countries, that facilitates trade and investment. Imagine what the economy of the US would look like, if each state determined its own rules for governing trade and investment across our borders. And child labor laws in other states. This is what we are facing on the world stage. The existence of the WTO, and our membership and adherence to its provisions, are an important reason for this country's growth in prosperity in the past half-century."

"The WTO was founded five years ago."

"I didn't know this was a trivia contest. I thought we were here to debate serious issues. I meant of course the WTO and its predecessor organization."

"I didn't know that a forty-five year historical gap was trivia. And to which organization are you referring?"

No answer.

"The General Agreement on Tariffs and Trade?"

Hall just stared.

"Or The United Nations' Generalized System of Preferences? Or what?"

Hall looked at his notes.

Sarah looked at her watch.

"But for you, Mr. Hall, I would be in my gym class now. I can miss gym for a good reason, but giving you a remedial lesson in history will not get me an excuse slip."

Hall's face was red.

"I stand corrected on the history of the WTO and ...the other organizations. And I maintain that their provisions have not only benefited American businesses, workers and consumers, but have also benefited our counterparts in other countries. The economies of all freely trading and investing countries are healthier."

Noll: "Economies don't live and breathe. People do. And the benefits that you refer to are distributed unevenly. In our country, some companies benefit from these agreements, some do not. Some consumers benefit, and some consumers lose their jobs to cheap foreign imports. And I think it would be even harder to demonstrate that workers in low-wage countries are benefited. Many of these countries are foully corrupt. Children and other workers are paid pennies to assemble products that are sold here for hundreds of dollars. Does my opponent really believe that the export earnings of these countries greatly benefit these workers?"

Hall: "This is unfortunate, really. But remember that their economies are very different from ours. Those small earnings may be enough to make the difference between eating and not."

Noll: "Of course. They are given just enough to keep them alive and working. Certainly not enough for food or school fees for their brothers and

3

sisters. The owners are enriched. Are we not talking about virtual slavery? Slavery in our country prospered at one time. The slaves were fed. The economy as a whole may have benefited. But the slaves did not benefit from this system. Their owners did. The analogy is good, because there is a virtually captive working class that includes children, in many countries with whom we are trading and investing.. And many children are literally sold into bondage. In our country, this was accepted for a period of time. But one man believed that there could be no economic justification for this moral outrage, so he did something about it."

"So my opponent seeks to assume the mantle of Abraham Lincoln and free the slaves in other countries!" he said, smirking.

The auditorium was still. There was a long pause as Sarah stared at her opponent.

"Mr. Hall, before you said that, I imagined that you were a person of good will, but possessing a limited ability to grasp the issues, and a having a profound ignorance of our topic. Now I see that I was wrong in the first particular."

Hall didn't reply for a moment. He looked as though he had been slapped, hard. Then he gasped, "I don't think that *you* have a grasp of the issues. You have simply stuffed your head with facts, to impress the judges!"

"You have unnecessarily elongated your sentence, Mr.Hall. You should have stopped after 'I don't think.' And I am sorry if you are uncomfortable with facts. But perhaps your illusions serve you better."

Hall was shuffling his feet behind the podium, as would a child in urgent need of a bathroom. His cheering section were starting to look like mourners.

Sarah continued. "I believe that there are absolute standards of moral behavior that transcend borders, and that our looking the other way when we know of transgressions that we would not permit to take place in our country, makes us a party to these injustices and cruelty. In some Latin American societies, there was an ancient practice of placing a young virgin on an altar, cutting out her heart with a stone knife, and then throwing her body into a sacred well. Should this practice be contemporary, it would cause outrage all over the world. But my opponent would accept it as a tolerated activity, by one of our important trade partners. Just a cultural difference, and none of our concern, he would say. But I would rather see one sacrifice like this take place, than know of the suffering, maiming and deaths of thousands of children under abusive labor practices, which in fact are going on as we speak."

Hall recovered. "I would, too. And I have in mind an excellent candidate for the sacrifice."

There were loud guffaws, hoots and cheers from Hall's supporters. Their champion was back on his feet. For a moment.

"I wasn't aware that your mind was attending this event, Mr. Hall. I thought you had checked it at the door along with your assault rifle."

The judges were doubled over in laughter. The Chancellor was holding his sides as he struggled to regain his composure.

Hall then understood that he had been set up, twice. His face was beet-red. He was furious.

"You're nothing but a quota fulfillment!"

Moderator: "Mr. Hall, a personal attack has no place in these proceedings."

Noll: "I accept Mr. Hall's statement. I was selected in order to raise the average IQ in this contest to an even one hundred."

The Chancellor was now looking at the floor, his face in his hands, as his shoulders heaved in laughter.

Moderator: "This Heckel and Jeckel exchange has been entertaining, but may I remind both of you that we are debating a substantive issue?"

Hall was desperate. He shifted gears.

"This country was founded on the ideal of freedom. What we are talking about here is the freedom of people and countries to buy and sell from each other, to their mutual benefit. Without these agreements, each country would be free to block imports, to protect their local industries. We would be back in the middle ages. When my opponent goes to the mall with her girlfriends, her baby-sitting earnings go further because her 'Hello Kitty' purse was made in China, not California."

Noll: "Freedom is indeed a beautiful ideal. But its exercise can often deny the freedom and rights of others. No one should be free to steal my bicycle. Children should not be free to play on railroad tracks. And feudal states should not be free to access our markets with cheap goods made by abused children. When my opponent buys the latest sports shoes that his heroes have endorsed, he has more money left over for his Pokémon cards because the child who sewed the shoes received less than a dime. If this is an ideal, what is an outrage?"

Hall: "It has been demonstrated time and again, that unfettered trade and investment benefits all. So the United States has put its support behind the WTO provisions. Each member country gives up something, but each gains. And the world community as a whole benefits."

Noll: "But the rules are applied selectively. Japanese consumers are still not permitted to buy our rice. This benefits Japanese farmers, but hurts Japanese consumers and our rice farmers who are able to produce rice at a much lower cost. American consumers are still not allowed to buy sugar on the world market; we are forced to pay three times as much to protect rich sugar farmers in the US. The WTO has changed nothing; the opportunists simply have a new set of rules to evade."

Moderator: "May we get back on track, please? The issue is child labor."

The debate continued, each scoring points, but with Sarah holding a commanding lead.

Moderator: "May we now proceed with a summation? Mr. Hall?"

Hall's cockiness, his arrogance, was gone. He had just been mauled by a pit bull with a sweet face and red ringlets.

"We are part of a global economy. This isn't the 1800's. We are the world's largest trading nation, and our businesses and our jobs depend on the continuation of our embracing the principle and practice of free trade. It has been well demonstrated, on both sides of the political spectrum, that the countries that trade freely, and welcome foreign investment, are the ones that are better able to provide for their people.

My opponent makes a big issue about child labor. In some rural areas in this country, children are excused from school at harvest time. Their work is needed. Is this slavery? In some countries, children's labor is needed for the family's survival. Who are we to challenge this?

Attempting to impose our will on other countries is a violation of their sovereignty, and additionally harms the American consumer who will be denied the right to buy products at a lower price.

My opponent's heart is in the right place, but her head is not. She wants to send gunboats to impose her ideals on other people's behavior. A free exchange of trade and investment, worldwide, is the best policy to optimize people's welfare. And that should be our goal.

Thank you."

Noll: "My opponent is probably the only person in this auditorium who hasn't heard that I have *not* stated an objection to children working. But I don't think that McDonalds beats its fourteen year-old employees or chains them to the griddle. I oppose the abuse of children in the workplace. Because that is where the United States can make its influence felt. And I have made it clear that I do not advocate the forcible imposition of our will on any country. My opponent missed that one, too. But we can withdraw our economic support. If the convenience store down the street mistreats its employees, sells scummy magazines or otherwise incurs my displeasure, I don't bomb it, I shop elsewhere. We, as a nation, have the right to shop elsewhere.

My opponent believes that 'free trade and investment' is an ideal that can be used to mask unspeakable horrors. I take the position, which has been well- documented, that the organized and pervasive abuse of children in many countries, continues. Slavery, the sale of children into bondage, the employment of six year-olds in textile mills, brickyards and nighttime places, continues. Boys and girls who should be in first grade where your children go to school are working twelve hours a day in factories that would send an OSHA inspector out the door screaming. Kids are blown to bits in fireworks factories masquerading as elementary schools. These are not simply my allegations -- they are facts uncovered by research by the U.S. Department of Labor. My opponent and the judges have been provided the documentation." Missy waved some papers for dramatic emphasis.

"We send troops across the world to smash armies that threaten our oil supplies. I don't want to send troops anywhere. I want the United States to exercise its greatness, its moral power, and its huge economic might to place sanctions on these countries, to correct their behavior, to make them stop rewarding their rich for maiming and killing kids. I want my country to just say 'no.'

My opponent has referred contemptuously to my baby-sitting money. That was a good guess. Yes, I baby-sit. Because I love children. And as much as I cherish every one of my children, I know that they are no more valuable in the eyes of God and their parents, than are kids in Pakistan, Brazil, India, Sudan, Colombia or wherever. They hurt when they are hit, they cry when they are hungry. They scream when their little fingers are torn off in carpet-making machinery." Missy made a wide and dramatic gesture. "But my opponent doesn't know about any of these things. He has failed to show that corporate interests in the United States should prevail over the interests of children who are suffering and dying all over the world, in the name of free trade and investment. He has failed to show that American workers and consumers are benefited by these abominable practices. He recites an empty liturgy, pulled from some Chamber of Commerce brochure, and absent of any concern for human values.

It has been said that all that is necessary for evil to triumph is that good men do nothing. I believe that my opponent is one of those good men. Well, I would like to introduce my gender to that fight, and to do something. Thank you."

At that moment, the buzzer sounded, signaling the end of her time limit. The judges noted Missy's precise timing.

A half-hour later, after the award ceremonies, Sarah was met by the Russian woman, her son, and the girl. Tears rolled down the woman's face, as she wrapped Sarah in a huge embrace. "You wonderful child! You beautiful child!"she cried.

"You did it, Missy!" chorused the boy and girl. "You won! You won the state championship!"

Then Theodore Hall III approached, some of his strut coming back.

"Miss Noll? I want to congratulate you. Really, you deserve the honor. No question. I'm sorry, but the personal stuff wasn't really against you, it's just my way. Maybe getting beat up was good for me." He extended his hand, and they shook.

"Thank you for being gracious, Mr. Hall. You did very well."

He asked Sarah to dinner.

"Thank you. But I'm with my friends, and we're going home tomorrow."

After Hall left, the Vietnamese-American girl and her parents shyly approached Sarah. The girl said, "You really did a great job! Congratulations!"

Sarah replied, grabbing both the girl's hands. "So did you. *You* should have won!"

The girl looked embarrassed, now knowing that Sarah had witnessed her humiliation.

"Can we correspond? I'm May Minh. Here's my name and address, and e-mail."

"Sure! I'll send you my address!"

The two girls hugged.

May's mother was gazing at Sarah as though she were a goddess. Her father put out his hand. "Thank you," he said, simply. He looked straight into Sarah's eyes as they shook. He understood. He understood people, and situations. That is why he had been a major general.

Sarah understood also. "Sir, it was my pleasure," she replied.

Then a group of grim-looking suits and gowns swept by, not seeing

Sarah. One said, "That Abraham Lincoln remark killed him. I thought he was smarter than that."

At dinner at their motel that night, the boy and girl presented Sarah with a framed caricature of herself, dressed as the biblical David getting ready to sling his stone, and captioned "Missy the giant-killer!"

"When did you do this?"

"Last week. We knew you were going to win!"

Missy started to cry. Her face went down on her folded arms on the table. The battle was over, and she was standing triumphantly at the top of the mountain, as Goliath lay dead.

CHAPTER TWO ————————————

THE FIRST TIME I SAW Missy, she looked like a painted wooden or stone icon placed at the bottom of a large boulder, on the side of the mountain, left by Tibetan pilgrims as a signpost. As I approached, I saw no sign of life. I had a feeling of dread. I was searching for a lost twelve year-old girl, and hoped that I would be the one to find her, to take her home alive, while dozens of searchers were looking in the wrong places. I didn't want to be the one to discover her body. I sidestepped up the steep slope, failing once and sliding down. Then as I started up again and grew close, I saw clearly a young girl in a red and blue ski suit sitting upright, cross-legged and motionless, grim-faced, her eyes closed. I shouted, "Missy! Missy!" as I approached, praying that she would hear and respond. She opened her eyes and looked at me, uncomprehending.

"Missy, I've come to take you home!" She appeared to be gazing at an apparition – who or what is this? Then she smiled slowly, a row of braces-clad teeth showing instead of the frozen grimace. Red curls spilled from under her yellow wool cap.

"Mister, I'm really cold!" she cried.

I'll bet you are, I thought. I took off my skis, and looked around. She was probably in the best-sheltered position in the immediate area; maybe that's why she survived the night. I decided to stay where we were for now. "Missy, up on your knees, please." I helped her up. I unzipped, and with some trouble, got off her ski jacket. Underneath she had a shirt and thin sweater. I opened my big coat and wrapped it around her, hugging her close, and rubbing her back. I was overheated from the climb up the hill; this is good heat transfer,

I thought. Get her body heat back. Her ears, fingers and nose seem ok. The toes are next, but can wait a few minutes. I remembered my cross-country skiing class, and reading about survival and rescue procedures.

I laid her back in my big coat, closed it, then took off her boots and socks. The socks went inside my shirt. Her toes were like ice but didn't look frostbitten; I thought I should have seen white spots if they were in trouble. I tucked her bare feet into my armpits, and clamped down lightly on them. It was awkward for both of us, but I really was concerned about her toes; I guess I knew then that I would be able to get her back to her family alive, and I wanted to return all of her, not just most of her.

She was still shivering, but looked better. After a while, I put the warmed socks back on her. It was about four in the afternoon. We could not get back to the hut tonight. It will be a full day's trip tomorrow. I was exhausted. How could I carry her? I knew I had to, unless rescuers found us tonight. Then a sudden thought: "Missy, where are your skis?"

She looked confused. "I lost them. I don't know."

I had read that hypothermia causes confusion. But her skis were nowhere in sight.

I cut off bunches of small spruce branches, and laid them on the ground, placing them in a depression in the snow to create a mattress under the boulder, then laid out the thermal blanket. I picked her up, and wrapped her in the blanket. She looked warmer. She kept her eyes on mine. Now and then I saw the flash of metal as she smiled.

I gave her an energy bar, and cautioned her to nibble it slowly: "Don't gulp it down!" I made her drink some water. I set up my tiny Primus stove, put some water in a small pan, and added some sweetened condensed milk. I sat her up and gave it to her in small, hot sips. When she had had enough, I finished the rest, and the remains of the energy bar. She gazed at me with a look of contentment, and adoration. Then she smiled gently and closed her eyes, the smile lingering.

"Missy, I am going to take you back to your Mom and Dad as soon as we can." She opened her eyes. The look was different. Her eyes went neutral. I wrapped her up tighter and cradled her head for a moment; her eyes closed, and the smile had gone. She slept.

I knew that the wind would be up tonight, and we needed some shelter. I wished that I had the lightweight shovel that many backcountry skiers carry, to make benches and snow caves. But I cut some snow blocks with my small saw, and piled them, then shoveled as much snow as I could with my hands to create a windbreak, with the boulder sheltering us on the other side. There wasn't much more I could do to improve the shelter, so I did what I could in the remaining light. I busied myself with my Global Positioning System device, noting our location, and going over tomorrow's route to the cabin. What if a storm were to come up? Well, we'd just have to stay until we had visibility. But - I've got to get this girl to a hospital, and soon. I placed a red flasher prominently before I bedded down.

I pulled the blanket around both of us, and then worked her ski jacket and my big coat on top. I felt for her toes again, still warm. We huddled together. And I slept. At some time in the night, I felt her stir. I dozed, and when I awoke for a moment, I felt her arms wrapped around me tightly, while she made heavy sleeping sounds. We were both warm. And we slept.

*   *   *

I awoke to something, a sharp sound. The shout of a skier? No, it's Monday, and they're at work or school. Maybe rescuers? No, just the wind on something, or a bird. But it was bright outside our blanket and snow cave. I saw Missy blinking at me, and her little smile as she remembered where she was.

"I'm going to get up and ready to go. You stay in bed." She smiled at the word "bed." I made some more milk tea, and gave it to her with another energy bar. And we both ate the rest of the bread and cheese.

"Breakfast in bed!" she smiled. Good, I thought. If she can keep up her sense of humor through all this, she'll be ok. I was starting to like this child. Well, I've saved her life; I'm being protective, that's all. But there was more. It was the way she looked at me.

We have a long way to go to the hut, I thought. The good thing is that it's downhill, then mostly level, only a few small uphill climbs. I didn't tell her the bad stuff. Now there are two of us on one pair of skis, and I don't know how I can do this. It will not be easy. But we must reach the hut today. It's going to be a real job to get off the mountain, to my SUV and the road. But one step at a time. At least we have shelter at the hut, and clearly we can't stay here.

We packed up everything. I put her small pack with a koala hanging outside, inside mine. I told her what we were going to do. On the steep slope down from here, we will both walk. It's too steep to ski, with you on my back. When we get down there, and I pointed, we will go by ski, and will walk only when we have to, like going over rocks. And we started out.

I hadn't anticipated how hard it would be. After we had walked and slid down the big slope, the ground and snow became too irregular to be traversed on skis. I had managed by myself, but couldn't do it with her on my back. So we plodded along, my skis tied together and looped over my pack, then I would put my pack on front, and she would mount my back. And we would walk until I was really tired. Then she would get down, and we would walk slowly, she stepping in my tracks. She is a real soldier, I thought. Not a cry, not a complaint. We continued this for about two hours.

Then we came to some flat and clear terrain, and I knew that we could ski this. My tracks from yesterday were still there, and unbroken. This would cover most of the way to the hut; the last leg would be through some confusing woods, and we would have to walk through.

I put the skis on, grabbed the pack, and Missy climbed on me. We were making better time now, but we still had trouble. There were spills, each one painful, and difficult in getting back up. I remembered how hard it was to fall alone; this was much worse. And I was concerned about her being hurt when I crashed. Then as we proceeded carefully, I had a stream of thoughts. There was the very real possibility that we wouldn't make it. All it will take is one big spill, or a wrong turn. But I was resolved to not let this happen. Everyone is out looking for her, just as when a child is down a well. All resources are mobilized, from everywhere. All stops are pulled to save a child. But now, there is no one but me to take this girl home. And if I never do anything again, I am going to succeed at this.

Then I slipped into a gully, and a small wave of snow followed me and covered my legs. I was on my back, my legs and skis a foot under me. I couldn't move. Missy had fallen clear; she scrambled over to me, cradled my neck, and looked into my face. She pulled on my neck as if to lift me up. I felt as I did when I had my first playground fight, when the big kid had sat on my chest. There was no way to move, no way to get up. My own weight was keeping me down flat, and my legs couldn't help me; my feet were bound to skis buried in a bank of snow.

"Can you reach my bindings? I have to get the skis off." She couldn't do it. "Can you dig down and find my feet?" It was hopeless.

If I don't get up, we both die tonight. I have things in place and always have, to take care of my family. The business, the home, savings and life insurance will take care of my family if I go away tonight. Many of my much-loved relatives have gone before, and I am not afraid.

But I will not let this young girl die. Dear angels, please help me to take her home! And I lay for a while, thinking and praying, while Missy crouched next to me.

She didn't understand. This is a little slip that he will fix; this big guy has saved me, and he'll get us out of here, and we'll get going again. And he'll make me warm again tonight. She didn't understand that we were both facing death. She stayed by me, waiting for me to do something.

"Missy, can you move over there, away from me for a while?" And she moved up the slope, sliding even more snow on me. I started scooping away snow above my legs. "Now, Missy, will you come behind me, and pile snow under my back, as I sit up?" So we worked at this for a while, she helping me to sit up, and to get close to my feet. I had one pole in my hand, but I still couldn't reach my boots. I was almost there. "Missy, can you come behind me and push my back up?" She pushed hard, and I was able to locate my right binding, and push the release with the tip of the pole. With a struggle, I was able to get my right boot out. "Keep pushing my back hard, Missy!" With one foot loose, I was able to work around to the left boot and ski, and get that loose, too.

Then I was on my feet, digging out the skis.

I gave her a great hug, and I kissed her for the first time. On her right cheek.

We got out of the gully, and rested. We both had some water, and sucked sweetened condensed milk from the can. That was all the food we had left, until we got to the hut.

I resolved to take no more chances on the skis; only where the terrain was really level and safe would we ski; otherwise we would walk. We made slow progress now, but safe. We continued this way for the rest of the afternoon.

Then we entered the forested area that surrounded the hut. We stopped for a while to rest, and I checked my GPS. We were very close, within a quarter mile. But we were on the east side of the mountain, and light was failing fast. We had to get through the trees. I had lost my tracks, but then remembered that I had walked this part anyway, yesterday. I kept checking our position, and knew that the GPS readings were accurate to within fifty to a hundred yards.

I saw the red flasher at the hut from about fifty yards away. Perfect, because the GPS put me pretty close, but I could have missed the hut, but for the flasher. We couldn't afford to lose any time searching. We were both really at our limits of endurance.

As I fished the padlock key from my pack, I had a momentary feeling of dread. I had thought of jettisoning the pack at one point; it was extra weight, and I didn't need anything that would slow us down. We had to get to the cabin before dark, or we were both dead. I had thought that this might be the small thing that would save us. But if I had dumped the pack, would I have remembered to first take out the key? Without it, we would as well be back in the gully in the snow.

Inside was as cold as outside. I started lighting candles and kerosene lanterns; anything for heat and light. I tidied up the bed and added the quilt. I helped Missy take off her ski jacket, boots and socks. "Missy, take off your ski pants and get under the blankets. Keep your other things on. I won't look." I busied myself with lighting the Primus stove, then went outside and got some snow and melted it in a large pot, and made some milk tea to start with. I took it to her, and she sat up to sip it. She kept her eyes on mine as she drank. I left the cup. "Finish that, but I'll fix something better."

But she was still shaking, nearly spilling the tea. I took it back, and supported her back with my arm, and fed it to her. Then I put her under the covers again, and she managed a metallic smile.

There was dehydrated food and trail food, but I needed something fast. I found a can of vegetable beef soup, and a small can of tuna, and some crackers. Perfect! I mixed the soup with water, heated it, and made kind of a mush with the crackers. I sat her up again, and let her eat with a spoon, out of the pan. She wolfed nearly all of it down. She lay down again. She looked warmer, but was still shivering. I had fantastic thoughts of a roaring fire, or even an electric blanket. Missy wouldn't take her eyes off mine. "You stay here." She smiled at this. "I'm going to do some stuff. Then I'll warm you up."

I ate the rest of the soup and crackers, and left the tuna for the next day. I checked the weather report. Nothing about the girl; now they were broadcasting only weather, as usual. I guess that the original advisory was out of pattern; it was news, not weather, but important enough to present at the time. Now that the searchers were looking only for a small body, the story had lost its immediacy. But we were going to see storm conditions tonight, and more snow tomorrow. I rechecked my map, and reviewed the route down where it would be difficult, where easy. Because I knew the route, there shouldn't be any surprises, and we should be at the base in about four hours. By myself, it would be about two.

We're going to have a triumphant return, Missy, I thought.

I wished that there were some way to contact the outside. I could imagine her grief-stricken parents already believing that their daughter was dead. I felt very good about what I had done. I don't always get things right, but now I have done it. With the help of the angels, I was careful to add in my thoughts. She is alive and well, and I will keep her alive and well, and she will not lose even a toe to frostbite, and I will deliver her to her parents, and she will be checked in a hospital for a day or two, and in a few days she will be back in school. She will use newspaper clippings from the Bellingham Herald to show her story, placed on a bulletin board in her school library, and then shown at an assembly in the auditorium, where she will be introduced by the principal to tell of her great adventure.

As for me? My wife will be angry at my not having returned as planned, and carp at my irresponsibility. She will have made plans to go out with her friends, that require me to be at home with the boys. "Do I have to do *everything*?" she will say.

I blew out the lanterns and candles, but one. Missy was still watching me. "Your turn not to look." I took off my ski pants and hung them over a chair. They were wet and icy, as were hers. I got in beside Missy. She was still shaking, so I asked her to lie face down, while I rubbed her back vigorously through her shirt and sweater.

"Thanks," she whispered. "That really feels good. But my feet are still awfully cold."

I felt them. They were like ice. I decided to do the feet and armpit position again. I turned her face-up, keeping blankets bundled on top, covering her lap and legs, with only her feet protruding. I nestled them in my armpits. And I waited while her small feet warmed. Her eyes were still fixed on mine.

"That really feels good," she said again.

I was exhausted and wanted to sleep. Is that why my mind played a trick on me? This position suggested a carnal possibility: that was the funny and fleeting thought that must have run across my face, because I saw the slightest smile and a flicker in her eyes as she understood too. I was struck that awareness had just passed silently between us: an innocent, -- do you see the humor in this that I do?

I blew out the remaining candle by the bed, then tucked all the blankets at the base of the thin mattress, and put the thermal blanket and our ski jackets on top. We lay like two spoons together in a drawer, with my arms wrapped around her. Our legs were together, holding warmth. She was not shivering now. But the wind was coming up, and finding cracks in the hut. And we slept.

In the middle of the night, I turned to lie on my back. She sensed the loss of warmth, and half awoke, following me with her arms and legs. She had one arm across my chest, and I had my arm across her back. One of her legs was between mine. Did I imagine she was squeezing me tight? Then we slept again.

We both awoke as a branch crashed onto the roof. The wind was howling now, some of it crossing the room. We hugged more tightly, and I wished we had more blankets.

Morning. Through the cracks in the shutters, I saw light. I checked my watch - it was after eight. We needed to get moving. I disentangled myself from Missy, got up and went to the door, and opened it a crack. The wind was down, but it was a blizzard. We were not going anywhere today. Even if the snowfall were to stop now, we would have too much soft, new, deep snow to traverse. I got back in bed. Missy was still sleeping.

The cabin was like ice. I saw the remains of our milk tea on the floor by the bed, frozen solid. My quick trip had me chilled, and I was glad to get back to the warmth of the bed and Missy. No hurry now, I thought. I'll make some breakfast after a while, from some of that dried stuff. I wonder what time the newspaper comes?

After a while she stirred, and sought me again. Her thin arms wrapped around me, and I held her again, and a warm leg was back between mine. She sighed and we both slept, our warm bodies pressed together, defending against the freezing air.

A little movement by Missy awakened me, and I opened my eyes to see her looking straight at me from only inches away. She smiled. I quickly squeezed her tight.

"Are you ok? Did you sleep all right?"

She nodded. "But you were snoring!"

"I'm going to fix something hot to eat. Ok?" I got up carefully, taking one blanket with me to wrap myself. I opened the door. It was warmer outside than in the cabin, but snow was still falling. The wind was down. I put on my boots, went outside, and lifted the shutters for our light.

I busied myself with the stove, melting snow. I looked at our menu choices. Fettuccini with a cream sauce, beef stew, chicken and rice...I chose scrambled eggs, and boiled some water and mixed it in. I set two places at the small table, then rummaged through the cupboard to see what else I could find for our breakfast. Grapefruit juice! There was a small can that we could share, once it was thawed.

"Missy, keep one blanket on, and put on your socks. And we'll have breakfast!" We sat at the table, and ate a lot. Between spoonfuls, she smiled to herself, as though thinking about the improbable adventure that she was in the middle of. Then I told her that we couldn't go anywhere today, and why. She took the news agreeably.

"But what will we do today?"

"Well, we've got some books. They look pretty interesting. I'll read to you. And you can read too. And I saw some checkers. Today will be fun! And tomorrow, we'll go home."

Something was wrong here. She's twelve. Why isn't she crying for Mommy and Daddy? She totally accepts being with this stranger, sleeping with him in an open-ended outing. I thought hard. Is what I am doing completely right? I'm alone with a young girl, in the same bed, while her parents are probably crying their eyes out, listening to reports from the search parties. Is there something else I could do? How can I attract searchers? I still had the red flasher on the roof. And I had put the second flasher in a clearing near the hut. But we didn't hear a plane or helicopter, or snowmobiles, or the shouts of skiers. They wouldn't be looking over here anyway. In a few days, I thought, they will be looking for me, and will be looking at this hut first. But when?

Can we sit here and wait? Can I go down the mountain alone, as soon as the storm is over, and bring back rescuers in snowmobiles? Is that the smart thing to do? Then I thought that, as an absolute, I would not leave her alone in the cabin. I could make pretty good time alone, even after the heavy snowfall. But this new snow, on top of a hard pack, means avalanche danger. I thought of yesterday's brush with death in the gully -- a small accident that nearly finished both of us. If I don't make it, what will happen to her, alone in the hut? When they find my body, they would have no reason to check the hut. Maybe they wouldn't know about the hut. I know. I'll put a big note in my pocket, giving the coordinates of the hut, and telling whoever finds me to go there, and get the girl. But what if they don't find my body for a week? Or if no one checks my pockets? No, I'll wait for the snowfall to stop, and we'll get out together. We'll go slowly and carefully, and we'll make it in a half-day. We'll get to my car, and then we will be ok.

She looked at me as I thought all these things. She sensed the worry. "Everything is going to be ok," she said. "We'll get out ok."

While I scoured the dishes outside with snow, she explored the hut. "Hey, look what I found!" It was an old-fashioned stereopticon, with a shoebox half-full of slides. "Wow!" She put it aside, and got out a box of checkers. When I finished cleaning, we sat down at the table again, and she spread out the checkerboard, with a practiced look and smile. I didn't *let* her win; she simply won. Every time.

I got out my small camera and its tiny tripod. I placed it on the table, and set the self-timer. We posed for several photos.

Missy started shivering. There was only one warm place. So I put her back in bed, and I piled on the blankets and quilt, with our ski jackets between, for insulation. And she was warm again. I made some hot, sweet milk tea. I checked the weather radio again, and again went over our route on the map.

Then I put on my cold, clammy ski pants and boots, and went outside. I got into my skis and went around a bit, trying to get a feel for moving on this big new snowfall on top of the old. I could see that it was going to be more difficult than before. I tried to see the route that we would follow to start, and went a hundred yards before I came back. It wouldn't be easy, but we have to do it.

Missy was sitting up a little on the pillow, looking at the slides. I had piled up several of the books beside the bed, thinking of what she would like to hear. Lee had chosen well, for a hut in the winter wilderness. He must have thought of stranded travelers, some day having to stay over. There were Robert Service and Robert Frost. And Jack London. And the *One Hundred and One Famous Poems*. And *The Wind in the Willows*. How long will we be here? I'd love to read this novel in its entirety to her. She will love the part about Mole and Rat being lost in the snowstorm in the Wild Wood, and being saved by stumbling on Badger's home, the door hidden in a snowdrift. I thought with envy of Badger's roaring fire in his well-provisioned kitchen.

Well, we had better read while we have light.

I brought the hot milk tea, put my blanket on top of everything, and got in bed. She put down the stereopticon. Was it warmth that she wanted? She looked at me, and with a little-girl bashful look, turned, moved close, wrapped her arms around me and pressed close. And I squeezed her, and felt a warm, sweet swell of love for this beautiful child, a feeling I had never experienced before

And I wondered: is this how a father would hold his daughter if she came to snuggle in the morning? Or is twelve too old for snuggling? Would he have the same feelings as I have now? I hug my boys so hard and often that I'm afraid that some day I might break something. But as pleasurable as it is, it's a guy thing. The look of adoration that I get with Missy's embrace is different. The beatific, braces-clad smile that I get when I push back the red curls and brush her cheek with a finger. Is this love? On her part, or mine? Or both? Or am I going mad?

Then I remembered my first visit to the hut, when I was on my sleeping bag on the floor, and heard the soft noises of love from this same bed, where Lee and Sherry had slept. And now Missy was wrapped chastely around me for warmth and affection, and the recollection and the juxtaposition made me smile.

"What are you laughing about?"

"I'll tell you some day!"

And we slept for a little while.

"You said you were going to read to me!" I awoke. "I saw all those books." We untangled ourselves, and lay side by side.

"Ok, but first, I don't have to read this one, I'll just recite. My mother asked me to learn this, just for practice, when I was small." And I told her about the "Owl and the Pussycat." And she smiled with joy at every line.

"But, and owl and a cat, how could they get married and...hoo!" She knew that it was a nonsense poem, but still wanted to explore.

"What would their kids be like?"

"Haven't you ever heard of a catbird?"

She giggled. "You're goofy!" And then I thought of the beautiful innocence of this girl; she wasn't thinking of the practical issues confronting a large bird and a housecat who wanted to couple, she was worried about the children.

I selected one poem from the Robert Frost anthology, "Stopping by Woods on a Snowy Evening," describing the author's winter ride in a horse-drawn carriage past a neighbor's wood lot, and stopping to watch the snowfall.

She put a hand on my arm, and looked at me with her love look again. Maybe I am giving her the image of the pony that every little girl wants? Can I take her to New Hampshire and give her a ride in a pony cart in the snow? What can I do to consummate this beautiful love? As if in answer, she leaned over and kissed my whiskery cheek. And I finished the poem:

> The woods are lovely, dark and deep,
> But I have promises to keep,
> And miles to go before I sleep,
> And miles to go before I sleep.

And she nestled close to me again, as if to say, let's take a snuggling break before the next poem. And I moved some red curls aside, and kissed her cheek gently.

After a while I picked up Robert Service and read parts of "The Call of the Yukon".

It was Tuesday afternoon. It was three days since either of us had bathed, and we had both done a lot of sweaty exertion. I like to think that we got smelly together, but a twenty-six year-old guy is going to go gamy much faster than will a twelve year-old girl. Anyway, it was time to do something about it.

There was a washbasin, and the small cooking pots. I heated the largest pot full of water, and put it in the basin. Then I melted some more snow, and left the warm water in a smaller pot. I had a small hand towel in my pack, and got it out. There was a bar of soap.

"Bath time!" I announced. She gave me a look of alarm. "Missy, I'm going to go outside for a while. Here is some hot water and soap, and this pot has some warm water, clean. Give yourself a good wash all over, and then rinse with this water. Then get back in bed before you get cold. I'll come back later, and I'll shout before I come in."

I walked around, and started scoping out our route down the mountain. The red flashers were still going strong. The snowfall had stopped, as the light faded. I looked at the deep snow covering my tracks of two days ago, and thought of the difficulty of going through that new layer, over the old. With Missy on my back. We can do it; we have to do it. But how much better, if a search plane or helicopter were to see the flasher, and check it out? Why isn't anyone over here? How much trouble to send a plane? I'm making us as visible as I can!

I didn't want another gully incident. I had learned that one mistake could be enough. The rule is "Always three shall you be" or something like that. The idea is that if there is an accident, one stays with the injured, while the third goes for help. The rules were not applying here. There are only two of us, with limited abilities. But we both have balls.

After a while, I went back to the hut and called for Missy. "Are you in bed?"

"Yes, ok!" she shouted.

I entered and looked at the basin and pot, both full of dirty water. I took them outside, emptied them, and started again melting snow. Missy was busy with her stereopticon.

I took the basins outside, carrying one blanket. It wasn't really cold yet, so I had my snow bath rubbing hard, then the warm water and soap, then scrubbed again with snow, then the clear warm water. I sang Italian opera. I felt really clean and virtuous. I put on my only change of briefs. I had packed for two days only, not expecting an extension of stay, and certainly not expecting company.

When I went in, wrapped in my blanket, Missy was still looking at the slides. But then I noticed her panties, freshly washed, draped over one of the chairs. "Missy, these won't dry here, because there is no heat. They'll just be icy in the morning. Put them in bed with you, with your socks, and they'll dry out from our body heat." And I wrung them out hard and handed them to her.

Uh-oh. Is she sleeping with no panties on? I was sure she didn't have an extra pair in her pack. Why should she, on a day outing? I swallowed hard. "Missy, do you have another pair of panties that you are wearing?"

"No, but I didn't want to wear the dirty ones after I took a bath, so I washed them." She kept looking at the Grand Canyon or something. She had her big shirt and sweater on. But there was nothing like a big towel or small blanket that I could give her to wear.

So I left her with her stereopticon, and marveled again about the innocence of childhood. I don't think that my hands wander when I sleep, but I have got to be careful, very careful tonight, because we are looking at potential trouble. Or should I make her put on her wet panties?

"My name is Hamlin. I'll be your waiter. Let me tell you about our specials for tonight. Your choice of chili and beans, fettuccini with cream sauce, chicken and rice, or beef stew." I wondered what the beef stew could possibly taste like.

"Can we have chili? That sounds great!" So I emptied the dried stuff into a pot of boiling water, and let it sit for a while. I set the table again. There was nothing else to drink, so I made some more milk tea. A feast for two hungry people. And I set the table, with a couple of paper towels, spoons, plates and metal cups. And a candle on the table, in the middle.

Missy got up with a blanket around her, and joined me for dinner. And all the while, as she ate enthusiastically, she now and then paused to give me a big smile, as if to say, isn't this a great adventure?

It was only six p.m. We would need a good night's sleep to get out tomorrow, but what to do this evening? I was planning a date. How will I entertain this lovely lady this evening? And how will I sleep with this almost-pubescent girl who is wearing no panties?

I got down *The Wind in the Willows* and started reading as we sat at the table. She listened, enchanted, as I described the meeting of Mole and Rat, and their adventures on the river. And we stopped for a while.

I took the pot and dishes outside and cleaned them with snow. She tried to help me to tidy up, but there wasn't much to do. She put the paper towels in our plastic trash bag. And then Missy was standing there in her army-brown blanket, looking at me.

I asked, "Do you like this story?"

"Sure. I want to hear the rest of it!"

So while she sat at the table looking at the illustrations, I made some more milk tea. My Primus was getting low on fuel. We needed to get out of here soon.

The book was an original, with the Arthur Rackham illustrations. Missy had scanned the book, and saw the scope of a very big and important story.

I continued reading for a while; she laughed at the meeting with Toad of Toad Hall, and his nonsense. Then I asked her to read. She happily took up the task. I noticed that she didn't stumble over a word. She smiled all the while, her eyes excited, as she was thoroughly taken with the delightful animals and their magic world on the river and on the road. We took turns reading until Missy started to look sleepy. I fixed up the bed.

"Missy, I'm going to turn around. Can you wrap yourself like a Tootsie Roll in your blanket, but leave your head and arms out?"

"Sure, but why?"

Gulp. "Because you don't have panties on, and I'm afraid your bum will get cold."

She accepted the explanation.

"In Japan, they have a saying, 'If your bellybutton isn't covered when you sleep, you are sure to catch a cold.' So maybe it's true of a cold bum, too!"

"How do you know that?"

"Because I lived there for a while."

"Wow!" As I looked away, she took off her blanket and started to wrap herself like a Tootsie Roll. I finished wrapping her loosely in the blanket, then picked her up and put her in bed, and covered her with the rest of the blankets. I put my blanket and our coats on top, and got in beside her. Then blew out the last candle.

We were quiet for a moment.

"Hamlin, did I do something bad?"

"No, you couldn't do anything bad. Because you," I said, finding her nose in the dark and squeezing it, "are a sweetheart!" And I could feel her smile as I gave her a strong squeeze and a loud kiss.

Then we settled into a warm snuggle as though we had been sleeping together for ten years. I hoped that she was dreaming of the animals on the river. I was praying that she would keep the blanket on, and wondering how we were going to get down the mountain on one pair of skis. And we slept.

*　　　*　　　*

It was early, and Missy was still sleeping. I checked outside; the sky was blue, and the wind down. But we would have to contend with the heavy powder snow on top of everything in sight.

The chicken and rice looked like the best choice for breakfast, so I cooked that, and made some more milk tea. I melted more snow, and filled our water bottles. We had a long way to go, and couldn't afford any mistakes. My instructor had said "It's a desert out there!" You must keep drinking water, just as though you are trekking the Gobi Desert.

Missy was still a Tootsie Roll, and I lifted her to her chair. And we ate a lot. I guess you can actually live on this stuff, I thought, though it would be great to have an apple or an orange.

I brushed my teeth, then cleaned the toothbrush, and put it in boiling water for a while. Then I gave it to Missy, and she brushed.

I arranged all of our gear, packing both of our backpacks, her small one going inside mine. Missy unwrapped herself from her blanket, and got dressed. I wanted to stay as light as possible, but we were down to the essentials. I left the little remaining food, but kept the can of tuna and the crackers, and what was left of the sweetened condensed milk.

We were ready. Missy was toying with her coat zipper, running it up and down. She had her back to the door. She looked at me. She had a big question.

"Do you like me?" she asked.

"Does a bear like honey?"

She gave me a big smile. The answer, and a quick hug, satisfied her.

We went outside, and I pulled down the shutters and locked them, then pulled the front door closed, and put the padlock in the hasp and locked it also. Missy clowned for one last snapshot. Then she was looking at me. I felt like Ernest Shackleton on his heroic rescue of his expedition from the ice floes of the Antarctic, nearly a century before. Then Missy climbed on my back, and we started out.

We sank six inches through the powder snow on top before hitting the old snow. This slowed us down. But we made progress down the gradual slope, down the mountain to the plain. We were making pretty good time now, with the occasional spill. Then I decided we wouldn't spill any more.

We couldn't talk, so my mind streamed to other places, other times. I was windsurfing in the Philippines. I was on Mindoro Island, in the small harbor town of Puerto Galera, which had been, centuries before, a safe refuge for the fleets plying trade between China and the port cities of Cebu and Manila. It was now a quiet tourist town, with bamboo huts on the beach renting for two dollars a night, beer fifty cents for a big bottle, and some Australians who rented small catamarans and sailboards for almost nothing. And every morning I got on a board, and into the ocean, sometimes coming into the harbor if the wind was up inside.

Well, windsurfing is much like skiing, in that you fall down a lot at first. But when you fall off the board, you not only have to get back on the board, but you have to haul the sail back up. It's a lot of work, so you don't want to fall.

One day, I sailed out in the harbor to escort the big wooden passenger ferry, to take over where the playing dolphins stopped; they would spin and prance and dive along the ferry on open water to the delight of the passengers, but would not go into the harbor. I was approaching the ferry, and then saw to my great concern that I was sailing over a coral formation; its sharp, thin spear-cones were only inches below the water. If I fell, I would be impaled like a burglar on the spikes and broken glass that the rich people in Manila have embedded in the top of the walls around their houses. And the incoming ferry passengers would see my sail like a big blue and yellow napkin floating on the surface, as a wide stream of red spread out with the current. So I didn't fall.

And I decided that I wouldn't fall with Missy anymore. We had had enough bumps and bruises.

Then we reached the plain.

I looked at an expanse of snow a mile long in front of us, broken only by an occasional stand of firs, and a small rise that we would have to cross. On another day, this would be an hour's pleasant exercise skimming along in the leader's tracks, or even breaking trail. Now, I was only sinking under the additional weight. Or taking off the skis, strapping them across my pack, and wading through the half- foot of new snow on top of a hard pack. When I got really tired, I would ask Missy to walk for a bit. We couldn't stop, I knew. But it was even harder for her than for me, so we had to go more slowly. It helped that she could step in my tracks. So this would give me some rest; we would continue this way, until I saw her tiring. Then she would climb back on me, and we'd keep going.

I knew that from the other side of the plain, it was downhill, and not far to the road. The danger from there would be avalanches. But now our job was just to cross the plain. After we had crossed the small rise, we stopped to rest in a grove of firs. Five minutes only, I told both of us. We ate the canned tuna, and drank some water. I knew that we could stay longer, and take a rest, and never get up again. We'd be packed out on search and rescue snowmobiles in two black body bags, when?

We were both too exhausted to talk. But when we looked at each other, there was always an expression of trust on her face, not a hint of "are we going to make it?" I said, before we headed across the last leg of the level stretch, "We're almost there!" She knew I was lying, and why, and accepted it. We hugged hard once, then she climbed on my back and we started across. I went slowly and deliberately. Then the snow on the hard pack got thinner; the wind had scoured it off. So I got on the skis, and we proceeded faster. As long as I could keep up some momentum, we were ok. We were able to keep going. We finished crossing the plain, and came to the ridge. Now we had to go down.

I stood behind Missy, my arms around her, and then pointed. "See that row of trees at the bottom of that ridge over there?" I asked. "Well, the road that we are going to is on this side of it."

She turned to me, smiling. "So we're really almost there!"

"Sure!"

My instructor had told us about the different levels of avalanche danger, the highest being "Extreme Danger." But most fatalities were in the "Moderate Danger" zones, rarely in the "Extreme Danger" zones. "Anyone know why?"

"Because no one is there!" said one guy.

"Right."

As I looked from the ridge to where we had to go, I saw no one. Well, it's Wednesday. But all the danger signs were there. And we have to go down.

I was probably breaking most of the rules, but no choice. We were going down in the middle of what looked like an arrangement of classic avalanche conditions. Lots of new snow on top of a hard pack, and starting to melt in the midday sun. I could only look for the best routes among many bad ones; I remembered to stay close to small trees, and to large trees that have branches close to the ground; these are the survivors. And we were able to avoid the obvious, scary, overhangs of snow threatening at the top of the ridge, and the "chutes" where overhangs drop their loads every winter.

I asked the angels to get us through this. You have done so much to get us this far; please don't lose us now!

Then the ground leveled out, and we were fighting our way through small trees and brush, and we went down a small slope that I thought looked like a road bank, and then I saw part of my red SUV, and I knew it was all over. And I took off my pack with the skis strapped on top, and picked Missy up, and hugged her.

"Let's go home, Missy!"

My car was the only one in the parking area, and it was nearly covered on one side with a drift. I rummaged through my pack and found the keys.

I scraped away snow on the lee side, the passenger door, and opened it. I climbed in, pulled Missy in and slammed the door. I climbed over the center, started the engine, and turned the heater up. I was glad I had a new battery.

I knew I couldn't drive out in this depth of snow, even with four-wheel drive; I could just make out the two-rut road I had used on the way up. I got my cell phone from the glove compartment. There was no response, as it was out of the service area. I wanted to stay here at least long enough to get Missy warm, then we could head for the road. I knew it wasn't more than a quarter-mile or so away, and would probably be clear by now. So we waited, and were warmed. I told Missy to get in the back seat, and lie down and rest. I reclined the driver's seat.

There had been no news on the weather radio for two days. I turned on the car radio, and tuned to the strongest station, which I guessed was Bellingham. There were the usual sports scores, commercials and crop prices. I was waiting for news. Are they still searching? I was exhausted. I dozed.

Then a news item came through ....

"A memorial service was held today at Our Lady of Lourdes Church for Sarah 'Missy' Noll, the young skier whose body was found on Mt. Baker on Monday. The brief prayer service was held at the request of Miss Noll's parents. Her mother said, "This service is for our daughter, but also to pay respect to the many searchers who tried so hard to save her life. We will always be grateful to them." The service was attended by the Mayor, and the Sheriff of Whatcom County, who directed the search. Miss Noll's parents will accompany the remains to their home in San Diego for final ceremonies."

I heard a desperate, pleading cry behind me. *"Hamlin!"* And a small crying sound, then silence. I was pinned to my seat by a heavy, terrible thing. I couldn't breathe. I was silently screaming and crying for Missy – then everything went away.

After a while, there was calm, and music on the radio. I forced myself to sit up and look behind me, to the back seat, expecting the worst horror of my life.

There was no one there.

There was nothing there but a tiny koala on a key chain.

I am going back up the mountain. This time, I don't need a backpack; I don't need food or water, nor a thermal blanket. I don't need a Primus, and I don't need a key for the hut. I picked up the koala and put it in my pocket.

I stepped outside the SUV, grabbed my skis, and turned to follow our tracks back up the mountain.

And walked straight into a snowball, which hit me between the eyes.

"Bull's-eye!" shouted Missy. "Got you with the first shot!" Then she flopped down on her back in the snow, kicking her feet, and laughing. She had built a small pyramid of snowballs while I was sleeping, and was lying in wait.

I dropped to my knees, and pulled her up. We locked in a hug, and we pressed faces. She wrapped her arms tightly around my neck. For minutes, we rubbed our faces together, as I affirmed her warmth and her life. I kissed her a dozen times. I bit her ear.

"Hamlin, did I hurt you? I'm sorry."

I couldn't answer.

"Why are you crying?"

I couldn't speak. I stood up and tried to look at the mountain, but saw only trees and scrub.

It was the most horrible dream of my life. And now Missy was standing next to me, her arm on my back.

"What's the matter, Hamlin? You were sleeping, and I didn't want to wake you up!"

"It's ok. I'm just glad that we're going home!"

I picked her up and put her on the hood of the car, and we hugged again for a while.

I put the skis and everything else we didn't need in the back of the SUV. I locked the car again, and we started hiking down, Missy on my back. After twenty minutes of wading through deep snow, we came to the road; it had been plowed to the width of one wide lane. We started walking down the road, glad to be free of the dragging snow, on a black track, the surface wet from snow melting in the sunshine. And in a few minutes we met a huge yellow snowplow on massive chained tires clanking up the road, and I flagged it down.

"It's the girl!" I shouted to the driver. She rolled down the window. "It's the lost girl! I need to get her to a hospital!" The driver was excited and was scrambling all over the cab. We heard her shouting on her radio.

"The girl is here! The lost girl!" Then she listened, looked at us again. "She looks pretty ok to me! There's a guy with her! I just found both of them! On the road!" She listened again for a while.

"This thing is too slow," she shouted. "They're sending a jeep for you from the ranger station. Here, wait up here, where it's warm!" We went around to the other side of the snowplow, and I gave Missy a boost up to the ladder to the cabin, then climbed up and sat on the seat, with her on my lap. She turned halfway and put her head next to mine, then rested it on my shoulder, as we sat enjoying the warmth of the snowplow cabin, and each other's close company for what we both knew would be the last time.

The rangers' jeep was there in a few minutes; it took us on a fast trip to the station, the driver being overly dramatic in his role as rescuer, careening into snow banks on both sides of the cleared lane. There was already a small crowd waiting. Behind the ranger station there was what appeared to be a small dormitory, where I guess the staff bunked, and it looked as though everyone on and off-shift had gathered, together with the few neighbors or visitors who had been able to venture that far after the storm. The news had spread fast in that tiny neighborhood. They all cheered as we drove in. Several people wanted to grab Missy, but I held her, feeling very proprietary. I set her on her feet. She grabbed me around my neck, and I picked her up; her legs went around my waist, as we were led into the Visitors' Center. Several women nevertheless managed to grab and hug her, almost tripping me, and a couple of them were crying over her, but I wouldn't let her go. Someone was taking photos. They sat us down at a meeting table, and then after a few minutes, brought some coffee for me, and hot milk for Missy. Then we waited for the ambulance.

The rangers on duty were asking lots of questions, without any order, and I told them that we were really tired, and can we talk later? I said that we were stranded on the mountain by the storm, and with God's help, we just got back down. I guess I sounded a bit impatient with them, but now that Missy was safe, I just wanted to rest. I was truly exhausted.

A couple of the rangers were pointing at a big map on the wall, and looking at me with questioning looks. I thought afterward that they were the first ones on the spot, and wanted to have the answers before anyone else did. Even up here, there are political forces at work, I thought. Besides the U.S. Park Service, there would be the state police, the local search and rescue unit, the sheriff's department, the local police, who knows what. No one wants to be left out; they all need recognition and funding. And I wanted to get up and help them, and I was unable to rise from my chair. I had exerted my body so much to save our lives, that I couldn't complete even this simple act. Missy is alive and well, and I don't have to do anything now, I thought. I've done it.

Missy was sitting next to me, taking little sips of her hot milk, while the women fussed over her. She looked a little bit uncomfortable, and grabbed my hand, and I held hers tight. And someone took another photo.

When the ambulance came, the attendants wheeled two gurneys up to the door. It hadn't occurred to me that they wanted me, too. I remembered my car. "I need to get my car out. It's snowed in at the top of the Wells Creek Road."

The guy who seemed to be in charge said, "Orders are, we get you both to the hospital, now. Your car isn't going anywhere."

"Well, you have my license number, anyway."

"Oh, you're the guy who goes to Lee's hut! Is that where you were?" I nodded.

I don't remember much after that. I do remember an attendant saying, "You two are the lucky ones. You wouldn't believe how many dead ones we give rides to. Skiers, snowboarders, avalanches, heart attacks." I fell asleep. When we arrived at St. Joseph's Hospital in Bellingham, I was wheeled to a private room, and lifted into a bed. I was given some hot soup. Then I fell asleep. I awoke a while later. I don't know what time it was. There were people around my bed asking questions, the press, I thought. I don't remember the questions or my answers. Then they went away.

A while later, I was awakened by a loud male voice outside, shouting, "Where in hell has she been for the last four days?" A woman's shrill voice was demanding, "Who is this person she was with?"

A few moments later, a female nurse came in with a large man in hospital greens, and two uniformed officers. They stood by my bed. "Hamlin Cross, you are under arrest for the crime of first-degree kidnapping. You have the right to remain silent…" And I felt one hold my arm down, as the other snapped handcuffs on my wrist, and around the bed rail.

CHAPTER THREE ————————

I HAD BOUGHT EACH OF the boys, Jason, six and Franklin, four, an angel. I had found them in a small shop in Seattle; they were about the size and color of a nickel, but oval-shaped and cast, not stamped, and appeared to be pewter or a similar alloy. They looked aged, but were probably new. One side was flat and blank, and the other side was an angel in bas-relief. While we attend church and Sunday school regularly, I placed no religious significance on the angels, but only asked that they keep them safe, don't lose them, and remember that an angel is with you. "Do they answer wishes?" I told them only that if you believe in the angels, they will be with you.

Today, Jason had Little League practice, in a big grassy field in a city park, not a regulation baseball field. While most of the twelve boys were doing a practice game with Coach Charlie doing the pitching, others were off to the side of the field doing batting practice with another coach. Their activities covered roughly the size of a small baseball field, plus another, smaller field for the batting practice.

It came time to go, about seven p.m., and the light was fading. As the boys headed for their daddies' and mommies' cars, and we packed up the balls, bases and other things for the trunk of Coach Charlie's car, Jason announced that he had lost his angel. "I had it in my pocket, and now it's gone!"

We started looking, but I quickly understood that with the size of the playing field, plus the side batting practice field, plus the consideration that all of this was covered with about three inches of grass, that the chance of finding Jason's angel was very slim. Still, we looked. I walked the bases, assuming that it fell from his pocket as we ran. He searched the practice batting area. We switched. One boy, who was left waiting for his daddy to pick him up, helped for a while, and then we were left alone.

It was quickly getting dark, and I told myself that this was not going to work. I didn't want to lose Jason's angel, but what was the chance of finding something that small in this large grassy field? I thought that I could get another at the same store. No. It wouldn't be the same angel. I told him that the angel would always be here when he practices, but we cannot take her home today. Then I thought what a useless explanation that was.

We crossed the field to the parking lot. I was tired of looking, and thought he was, too. I didn't think that he was very much upset at his loss, but as we reached the car, Jason broke out in little sobs, saying "Dad, can't we go back to look some more?" There was almost no light left. We can't find it. It would be a nearly impossible task to find the angel in daylight, even if it were a proper baseball field, not one covered with heavy grass. I'll come back tomorrow, when the boys are in school, and try again. But Jason wanted to go back to look, now.

We alternated walking the bases in the main field, the shortstop position and the fielding positions that he had played, and the batting practice area. Then, I decided that unless I knew where the angel was, there was no of hope of finding her. I will ask the angel where she is. I don't know how to do this. I closed my eyes, and asked, quietly, for direction. And did this for a few moments. And when I opened my eyes, I was directed with certainty in a line; I looked carefully as I walked. I went far enough that I knew that this wasn't it; it was too far out in left field, approaching the trees that bordered the lake, and I knew that Jason hadn't been that far out. So I retraced the path that I had been shown, and picked up small rocks, pieces of foil and other small things, and picked up another one, and it was the angel, face up. I held her up and shouted "Yo!" to Jason, and saw him run across the field to reclaim his angel.

"How did you find it?"

"I asked the angel to tell me where she was."

"Did you hear her talk to you?"

"She told me where she was through her thoughts and my thoughts."

At the dinner table that night, as we discussed how each boy can keep his angel safe, like putting her in a plastic bag with a safety pin, we came back to the topic of how the angel told me where she was. Then Jason reminded me with a shout that, "I *told* you that we should go back to look some more!"

And I was struck with the thought that if the angel had spoken to me; she may have also spoken to Jason!

We both told Franklin, who was listening to all this with wonder, that if you believe in your angel, and you listen to her, then she is real, and is with you.

I guess that you would have to see this grassy field, Waverly Park, in Kirkland, Washington, especially in fading evening light, to understand the near impossibility of finding a small object in the large playing area that the boys had covered. Luck, coincidence, or what? I prefer to believe that our angel wanted to be found, and did what only angels can do.

But this was to be only the first of many encounters with the angels.

CHAPTER FOUR ────────────

I HAD RECEIVED A BA in Electrical Engineering from the University of Texas, San Antonio; the four years had been crammed into three, as I carried a full load, and enrolled in the summer quarters. I was in a hurry to get on to the exciting stuff in life. I had then gone, on mostly a lark, I guess, to a small Japanese university for a two-year program terminating in an MA in Japanese Studies.

The first year was nearly nothing but language study. But on school holidays, the summers, and in the second year, I explored the country on a slow train, with friends or alone, and saw the scenes that looked like fairylands; tiny villages surrounded by rice paddies and vegetable gardens, and on the outskirts, neat and rustic wooden farmhouses and outbuildings, and in season, persimmon and apple trees outside the houses, with bright orange and red fruit decorating the still life of each little farm. I shared slow trains with giggling schoolchildren and old farm women with huge baskets of vegetables on their bent backs. And there were weekends at hot springs in the winter, where I went by train and bus to volcanic areas all over, and where I would soak with friends in steaming water outside the lodge, sipping on hot sake, and watching the big snowflakes gently falling on the water and on us.

And sometimes I would have a beer in a tiny bar, with construction workers who would laugh uproariously at my every utterance. A long-time foreign resident of Japan had told me: "To them, you are a talking dog. The wonder is not that the dog speaks so well, but that it can speak at all!" But they would not let this dog pay for a single beer.

One day on a train, I sat opposite a young woman with a baby boy on her lap. He was covered, but for his head, in a white blanket that fell on all sides around him like a poncho; he looked like a tiny and beautiful king. Seated next to them was an ancient farmer, with a gnarled, weather-beaten face. He sat quietly and stolidly, looking straight ahead. Then the baby slowly turned his head toward the farmer, gazing up at him. A smile creased the old man's face, and his eyes came alive. As the baby continued to gaze into the farmer's face, the leathery, wrinkled face erupted into a massive, gold-toothed burst of joy.

Another day I saw a girl, maybe sixteen, with her school friends. Her face was possibly the most stunningly pretty that I had ever seen. In another place, she would be a supermodel. They all got off at a rural stop; with the crossing bells clanging, they rushed off with their book bags swinging and their school uniform skirts waving. I hoped that she would never move to Tokyo, Osaka or New York, and that she would preserve her beauty, and have beautiful children, in this green, rainy, mountain-shadowed and quiet place.

One blustery winter day, I shared hot chocolates with fourteen year-old twins, a boy and girl. We were in a coffee shop in an alley near the sixteenth-century Matsumoto Castle, which we had just toured. We talked at length about many things. As we left, the girl told me, "You know, this is the first time we have ever talked to a foreigner!"

I saw the ugly side of the country, too. A friend's boat was sunk at its mooring one night, because he declined to pay for protection. And another, a coffeehouse owner, told of what happens if they don't pay. "The hoodlums will come in, and take over all the tables in the front. They will use loud and rude language, put their feet up on the chairs and tables, and insult anyone who comes in. So no one comes in."

A bar owner told me that he didn't have the choice of beer distributors. You buy from the one that the mob has claimed for this area. And what happens if you want to switch to another? "When he makes his first delivery, the driver will be greeted by three guys who explain things to him. If he returns, and he probably won't, he will be roughed up. There is rarely a third incident, because when someone dies, the police take notice. But not before then."

I was graduated. But what to do? I enjoyed being in Japan, and I loved the academic life, there and in the U.S. I often thought of teaching, and had been looking at the possibilities, during my second year. But you don't teach either of my disciplines with only a BA or MA, and I didn't have the money to continue for an advanced degree.

I thought of staying on in Japan to teach English. Most foreign students did that part-time anyway; the money was good. But there was no future. These were not structured English classes for the most part, it was really conversation practice, and the only requirement, whether freelance or as an employee of a commercial English language school, was a native fluency in English. A college degree and a white face got the best jobs; blue eyes and blond hair commanded a premium, whether male or female. I sympathized with my Japanese-American, Sri Lankan and Indian friends or any people of color, however perfect their English, who got the lower-paying positions or none at all. "English teacher", in Japan, meant a white face. And a passport from the U.S., Canada, a northern European country, Australia or New Zealand. None other will do. I was ok, but didn't get the premium for blond hair and blue eyes.

But the students who couldn't give up Japan, and stayed on to become English teachers, unless they were with an accredited public school or university, were usually headed for a dead end. It seemed that whenever a foreigner made the news in connection with a criminal act, his or her occupation was usually given as "English teacher."

So I returned to the U.S. And got married. And Jason and Franklin came along almost immediately after, because my wife's sister died, leaving two boys, four and six.. Her ex-husband had disappeared years before. And the day that Jason and Franklin appeared on our doorstep, long before the adoption papers were completed, they became my boys.

Now I had a family to support. When I arrived in Seattle, I had answered an ad for a "trainee in security systems installation" and listing the requirements as a vocational school certificate in electronics or the equivalent. I had learned something about alarm systems in one course in San Antonio, and thought that this could be a career. Having the practical experience would be only a springboard to starting my own business. I had a plan.

"You're overqualified! You're a graduate electrical engineer!"

"Look at my MA. Consider me a liberal arts grad. I just happen to have the electrical and electronics knowledge also."

We came to a compromise. They would take me on as a trainee for six months only, at the trainee pay. It was a good thing I had some savings left from Japan. After six months, I would go into management on the marketing side, or we would say goodbye.

So I started as a trainee. And separately, I incorporated "SOUND Home Security" and applied for an electrical contractor's license that would permit me to do "low voltage" work, meaning that I can't wire your home or your

220volt clothes dryer, but I can do burglar and fire alarm installations, and communications cable. I am an electrical engineer, and an electrical contractor, but not an electrician. To be qualified as the latter, I would have to start as a union-sponsored apprentice electrician, and take years to become a "high voltage" electrician. There was a better way.

I moved into sales and management. The money was good. But after a year, I hit the ceiling. It was a small, family-owned company, and I was not going to go higher until someone died. And so I resigned, and activated SOUND Home Security. I targeted the residential and hi-tech industry cities east of Seattle, across Lake Washington, away from my former employer's customer base, and we moved from Seattle to Kirkland. I couldn't afford to advertise, except for the Yellow Pages, so I spent most of my time knocking on doors.

The company name was a double-entendre for Puget Sound, the body of water flanking Seattle, and "sound" as in "safe". I was surprised that no one had co-opted the name. It seemed pretty obvious, I thought. And years later, when my wife and I reviewed our grand adventure, we guessed that an angel had been sitting on that name in the state registration office and so inquirers were told it was taken; and the same with the registration of the name on the Internet. The domain name was clear for me. It was mine for thirty-five dollars.

The logo was a deep blue "SOUND" in all capitals on a slant with bars above and below, and "Home Security", level, in black. On my truck lettering, there was a small brown owl with big eyes sitting on the crossbar of the "T" until someone reminded me that most burglaries take place during the day, when owls are asleep. So I retired the owl.

I was twenty-six. The business had been going well, steadily growing, for three years. I had college and high school students helping me knock on doors. I had alliances with real estate agents, locksmiths, anyone who talks to homeowners. There were two vans with ladders on top, and orange cones on the bumper for our installers, and to take the students around. I was working nearly every night; that's when my sales manager and I would visit customers, by appointments generated by the kids or our alliances, and make the sale. The installers would do their work during the day, with my filling in when we got busy. It was good for everyone.

My free time on weekends and the occasional evening was for the family. My wife had her circle of friends, and she would be out many evenings until late. A girl who lived at the bottom of our cul-de-sac watched the boys until

I got home. We would have a family dinner out once a week. On weekends, I would take the boys on day hikes or on a bicycle trail when they didn't have a soccer or baseball game, and now and then all of us or just we three guys, would climb into the big SUV and get on a ferry and go to an island or a peninsula, for a Saturday night stay at a B&B or a hotel. In season, we would go to Stevens Pass and put the boys on skis for a couple of hours, then stay over in the faux Bavarian village of Leavenworth, for snowball fights, and for some roasted pork knuckle, sauerkraut and potatoes, and to watch the boys dancing ineptly but enjoyably to the tunes of the smiling German accordionist.

Those were good days. But there was something missing.

Chapter Five ────────────────

One day, I received a catalog from Bellevue Community College. I hadn't asked for it; it just appeared. BCC was a local two-year college, offering additionally non-credit evening and weekend courses in a variety of academic and nonacademic subjects. The catalog's arrival was serendipitous: I was looking for something to do, out of the pattern, the routine of my life. I could give up an evening a week, or a Saturday morning.

As I leafed through the catalog, a course on cross-country skiing caught my eye. I'd never really thought about skiing; in Texas it's not very practical, and in Japan it's pretty expensive, for a student. Downhill skiing looked like fun, but I couldn't afford a broken leg or broken anything else. I love the beauty of quiet wilderness; Washington had plenty. And I needed the exercise. I signed up for the course.

It was for four evenings of classroom instruction, and two Saturdays or Sundays on the slopes not far away. At the first class, all the students introduced themselves, and their skiing backgrounds.

"My name is Randy. I've been downhill skiing since I was six, and I'd like to take up cross-country for some variety."

"My name is Sheila. My husband and I have done some cross-country, but we want to learn the telemark techniques, and decided to start with this course."

"I'm Myron. I've been XC skiing for a few years, but I'm sure I can learn a lot from the course."

And so on, around the big table.

My turn. "My name is Hamlin. I've never been on skis in my life."

At the second class, we had been asked to bring XC skis and boots, even if rented. The instructor had us boot up, fix our skis, and go outside the classroom to the wide student lounge, on the carpet, and practice the basic sliding movements. Kids were sitting at the round plastic tables and chairs, studying, drinking coffees and sodas, some chatting quietly, and ignoring this unusual procession of mostly middle-aged persons circling them on the periphery of the lounge, shuffling along with their skis and poles.

And I fell down. I fell down right in front of the table of a thirty-ish couple, who starting laughing uproariously. What skier falls down on a carpet? Red-faced, I picked myself up, skis clattering, my poles waving and just missing their coffees. "Well," I said, "I've never been on the slopes before." And that started them again.

Just then, the instructor announced a ten-minute break. I poked my bindings with the tip of a pole, to release my skis. The couple were still giggling, and couldn't stop. He was a rich- looking guy, slim, tanned and wearing good casual clothes. She looked like a trophy girlfriend. She said, "Please sit down with us. We're really sorry for laughing!"

He gestured toward an empty chair, still unable to stifle the giggles. "Ok," he said," finally settling down. "But we're both skiers, and we were talking about last weekend at Stephens Pass, and our misadventures, including lots of spills, and suddenly you came skiing past us on the carpet, and…" And they both started laughing again, she collapsing into his lap.

After they had calmed down, both still flushed, they introduced themselves. He was Lee, she Sherry. They were here because he was teaching an evening course in investments. He didn't say what he did otherwise, but he looked as though he didn't have to do anything. Sherry was vaguely "in real estate." I told them what I was doing, and my sudden interest in XC skiing. Lee told me that he was really enjoyed XC skiing more than downhill, but Sherry liked downhill.

"It takes so much less effort!" she said.

The break was over. They both wanted to meet me again. For their entertainment? They want to see me fall down again. Lee and I exchanged phone numbers. A courtesy, I thought, an apology for laughing at me.

A couple of weeks later, I had a message from Lee on my message pad at work. "Call me," it said.

I returned his call. "Hamlin, have you got your legs yet?"

"Depends on what you mean. We had our first class on snow, last Saturday, at Snohomish. So now I fall on snow. It's softer, but harder to get up. I sort of miss my carpet."

He laughed. "Well, let me know when you want to go out. Sherry and I and some friends go up to Snohomish pretty often for a day, or up to Stevens Pass when we have a couple days and can stay over. When we have more time, we go up to a place on Mt. Baker that I'll tell you about some time. We're not really all that good, though some of the guys are, and Sherry is really better than I am. But you won't feel out of place, I guarantee."

"I'd like that. The day trip sounds good. My wife isn't into skiing, though I'm trying to interest her. But I can take a day off, no problem."

"Ok! You're in Bellevue during the day, right? Let's have lunch, and plan something."

So we had a sandwich lunch, and we planned the next Saturday on some groomed track, logging roads that had been pretty well run over. I guess they chose this out of consideration for their novice skier. .

In preparation for doing some serious skiing on a long-term basis, I had returned the rental stuff and outfitted myself, following the recommendations of the teacher. I bought the skis, bindings and boots, and had the bindings mounted. I got the poles and accessories, plus some pants, gloves and liners, and tethers to keep your skis from running away down the hill if you and they get separated. I needed a cap. It was the busy season, and lots of the stuff was going fast, so I couldn't get a decent-looking cap; the only one in my size was a black one with the figure of a downhill skiing samurai embroidered on the front, and two large tassels hanging on either side. I would look like the Emperor's court jester with this, I thought. But I can always cut off the tassels, I thought; but for some reason, I never did. The cap was a great conversation piece when skiers gathered around their packs and got out the hot chocolate; I should have had it when I was single. And it was always good to get Lee and Sherry giggling again.

After my first day of skiing with Lee and Sherry, we headed back to Seattle. We stopped to get something hot to eat before getting back on the highway to the city.

While we ate our hot soup, Lee told me about other trips that they did. For an overnight, they would go by themselves, or with friends, to Stevens Pass, farther north, and too far for a day trip. There were lodges there, so it was convenient.

Then he told me about his hut near Mt. Baker. "You can't call it a cabin, because it's really only a shelter. It's an enclosed cabin in terms of the structure, but it has no amenities, like power, water or even a stove. It's in a designated wilderness area. I put in a kerosene and wood-burning stove a year ago, but the problem is getting a wood supply and keeping it dry, under snow, and transporting kerosene. It's pretty remote. And, because there is a flue problem that hasn't been fixed yet, there is danger of carbon monoxide poisoning. So we don't use the stove at all. The problem is the cabin's remoteness. The only way we could get people up there to do work is by snowmobile; but it's hard to do any work in the cold once you get there. In the summer, the workers would have to hike up, and there's not much enthusiasm to do that. So when I can afford a helicopter, I'll get it into being a proper cabin.

Sometime, we'll do a trip up there, so that you know where it is. I keep a padlock on it, but you can use it when you want. Just let me know ahead of time; it has one bed, only, and ok for two people only if they are the best of friends. Other visitors need to pack a sleeping bag. The good thing is that it is in the middle of some of the most beautiful backcountry skiing country you have ever seen. I'll stack it against Colorado any time. But nobody goes there, because of the access problem. It's in the Mt. Baker National Forest, and from the access road, you can park not too far from there. It is a four-hour trip up to the hut, and about two hours down. So you can do the whole thing in a day, once you get to the Mr. Baker area." I knew Mt. Baker was a half-day driving from Seattle, so it would really be a three-day trip, counting two nights and a full day of skiing from the hut

The cross-country season for Washington up to the Canadian border was really over in around May, so we wanted to get as much skiing in before spring. In the higher elevations, like on Mt. Baker, it was longer. But Lee said we should get up to Mt. Baker soon. He wanted to show off his hut, and his mountain. So we planned a three-day trip.

They came to my house very early on a Friday morning, and I served a big breakfast. Then Lee, Sherry and I got in my SUV. We were on our way.

The early Friday traffic was light; the crowd heading for Canada for the weekend wouldn't get started for a few hours. It was all four lanes, big trucks, and cars with skis on top, pretty clear driving, and not much scenery, for the almost two-hour drive to Bellingham, and the intersection with Route 542 heading east to the National Forest and Mt. Baker.

Now the scenery was small and large farms, and houses, and junkyards, and signs announcing plumbers, chiropractors, mystics and this Sunday's church services. Then sweeping farmland then gave way to the forest, and gradual elevation. We made a quick stop after we crossed the Nooksack River; Lee and Sherry wanted to show me the river. We walked down from the bridge, and started up a hiking trail by the side of the river. It was glacial runoff from one of the Mt. Baker glaciers, Lee explained. It ran through old forest, heavy with fallen trees draped with greenery, and massive straight firs. It could have been a rain forest, I thought, except for the cold and brisk wind.

We continued to the ranger station in the small town of Glacier. "We always leave a flight plan, just in case," Lee told me. "Then on the way down, we check out. It's not a requirement, just a good idea. Especially if you are by yourself. It's not a good idea to go alone, but I do it myself, so who am I to talk. I won't give up a chance to ski just because Sherry and everyone else is busy."

We sat at a table in the visitors' room in the ranger station, and we laid out my topo map. Lee marked where we were, where we would park, and the location of the hut. He wrote down all the coordinates on the margin of the map. A couple of the rangers looked on with interest. I wondered what they did on their time off. I knew that many people took this kind of job just to be where they wanted to work, and to spend their free time. It couldn't be for the money. Lee said, "The only real danger is getting lost. And avalanches on the lower part." He pointed at the map, an area of steepness just above where we would park. "But you know about the advisories, and you'll get up to date when you stop here. And your course told you how to spot obvious dangers. And you won't get lost, because you have your GPS and topo map. It's a good idea to carry a thermal blanket. It doesn't take much space in your pack, and it's light. But if you do get stuck overnight, like in a whiteout, it can save your life."

Then we were on our way. We made one last stop, at the eighty-eight foot-high Nooksack Falls, a short drive off the main road. Then we turned up a bulldozed road, drove up through the firs for about a quarter mile, and then turned into a small cleared area to park.

At first, it was a struggle against brush, small trees and steep slopes for the first few hundred yards, so we carried our skis. Then the terrain leveled off, and we put on our skis. We saw a wide expanse of almost unbroken snow.

"When we get across the plain," Lee said, "we'll be almost there." Counting a half-hour lunch break, it took us about four hours.

Lee was right. It was a hut. "It was put up here years ago, before the National Forest was established. Its origins are uncertain, but it must have been used by timber surveyors. The owners of the land kept rights to an acre of land, where we are, but never put anything on it, just left the hut. I got it for almost nothing, from an estate sale, a member of the family who owned the timber company. I made it structurally sound, but no really useful improvements, yet. The stove doesn't work. The flue is bad, and I need to replace the vent. That's why there's no fuel. So we've got good shelter, but no heat."

There was one small bed, with blankets piled on it. Right, I thought, you'd have to be pretty good friends to share it. There were basic utensils, a washbasin, some pans. Some cabinets held emergency food, candles and kerosene lamps. There was a shelf with some board games and a small collection of books.

We had brought some canned food. I had carried a bottle of burgundy, and Lee's contribution was a half- bottle of good port.

After our dinner of soup, bread and wine, and apples for dessert, we poured the port into tin cups. "We don't party much here," Lee said. "Our nearest neighbors are the Mt. Baker commercial skiing area, with lifts. A couple of lodges, the usual. It's about four miles away in a straight line, but seven miles if you're going there on skis or snowshoes. We are well outside the designated ski area, so we never see anyone over here. That's why we like this place."

Lee went outside to close the shutters when it got dark. When we finished the port, and the candles and lamps went out, I stretched out my sleeping bag. The hut was too small to hold secrets: love sounds came from the small bed next to me.

And then we all slept.

Chapter Six ───────────────────

I KISSED THE SLEEPING BOYS and left Kirkland very early, for a three-day back-country skiing trip on Mt. Baker. It was a four- hour trip to the trailhead. As long as I got there by noon, I would have a clear five hours to get up to the hut. This was my third trip to the hut, my second alone.

This would give me a full day tomorrow to go across the mountain; I had never encountered other skiers on our side of the mountain, though Lee said that there were occasionally wilderness skiers and snowshoers who found their way there. This was real back-country skiing. I remembered what Lee said about skiing alone. I was breaking the rule. But I was careful and avoided obvious risks. I thought that getting lost would be the worst danger, so I frequently checked my GPS readings against my topo map. I will not get lost; lost means dead.

I reached the hut early, about five p.m. Sleep would come easily tonight. I unpacked, straightened out the small bed, and arranged blankets and the quilt. I heated a can of heavy soup, and ate it with a big piece of bread, and an apple. Then I turned on my weather radio. It was a handheld receiver that looked like a walkie-talkie, but received only US Weather Service reports; I had programmed this one for the closest station. If it were left on, there would be a running commentary on temperature, humidity, air pressure and such, and forecasts. No news, music. Just the official weather people talking. Or if placed on standby, to conserve battery power, the radio would come to life if there were an alert.

But tonight's report was out of pattern. A twelve year-old girl was lost on the mountain.

She had been in the commercial skiing area, far to the west from here. The report had been put on the weather radio, to seek the assistance of any listener in the area who could help with the search.

I got out my topo map again. The area where she had disappeared early today was four miles away. I left the radio on. The searchers were probably fanning out in circles from where she had last been seen.

Then it came back to me. A true story, read in my childhood. A twelve year-old boy had become lost on Mt. Katahdin in Maine. All possible searchers were gathered; rangers, police, timber company people - all were out looking. They had set up support camps, with horses hauling in food and tents. Tracking dogs looked for his trail. The searchers found nothing. Because they were all looking in the wrong place. They had assumed that the boy had perished on the cold mountain, and their job, after a couple of days, was to recover his body. What really happened was that the boy got off the mountain within a day, and was below the killing cold, in the wilderness forest to the north of the mountain. He found a stream that led to a river, and knew to follow it to civilization. And nine days from his disappearance, he emerged, barely alive.

He wrote a book about his adventure; I got it from the school library. I was about ten. And I did a show-and-tell at school, after constructing a big papier-mâché relief map to illustrate. And I had examined the map, and the accounts of the searchers, and remember thinking that if the fishermen staying at the camp where he ultimately appeared, had thought that, it's a long shot, but what if he *had* gotten off the mountain, and was following the stream down, as a Boy Scout would know what to do, that he would be stumbling down the Wassatquoik River to the north of us, and why don't we go up the river and meet him? No one else has found him, and the National Guard and their airplanes were searching, but what if, just what if, he had got off the mountain and is headed this way? What else have we got to do but fish and drink beer? And no one thought to take this long shot, so the boy, Donn Fendler, got out by himself, and went to Washington in 1939 to be received as a hero by President Roosevelt.

As I looked at the topo map again, seeing my position and where the girl was last seen, I thought that it is a really long shot. This is just too far.

I kept the radio on. The reports went back and forth between the routine weather commentary, and the latest on the search for the girl. Helicopters were on the way from McChord Air Force Base, equipped with searchlights so that they could continue looking into the night. Some tracking dogs had been brought in, but still no girl. She had vanished.

Then a report described her as a twelve year-old cross-country skier! I jumped. Why didn't they say so before? A hiker or a downhill skier couldn't have gone far from the lodge and the lifts. But a cross-country skier could have covered a great deal of distance. I looked carefully at the topo map again, and saw that between the ski lifts and where I was at the hut, here was clearly a possible route along a path of little elevation change. This didn't mean that she had a clear course; it could have been blocked with rock outcroppings too small to feature on the map, heavy forest, or small gullies that would stop her. But I thought of Donn Fendler again. And it came back. Everyone is looking in the wrong places. What if one person, or a party, thought of the possibility that she had covered ground to the east, in a near straight line, and had most of a day in which to do it? While the distance between the hut and where the girl was lost was four miles, the winding around the mountain features would mean double that distance.

It *was* a long shot. But I am the only one here. I will go to the west as soon as I have light, and meet her. What else have I got to do? I came here to ski! And with the greatest of luck, if she survives the night alone, I will find her tomorrow.

I plotted my route carefully that night. I assumed that she would not try to gain elevation. But she would not have gone down, either; the slopes were too steep for a young child to maneuver. And if she had somehow gone down, she would have run into the Mt. Baker Highway. So my idea was that she may have come straight across, disoriented, and I would find her.

There were things to pack. A thermal blanket, a Primus stove with extra fuel, a can of sweetened condensed milk, some energy bars, a block of cheese and a big piece of bread. I had two red flashing lights; I packed one to signal for searchers, and placed one above the door of the hut. I put in a lightweight saw and two full water bottles. Then I set out for what would be at the least a good day of skiing, and if the angels are with us, the rescue of a dying little girl.

Six hours will be about my limit, I thought; if the route is as clear as it looks on the map, it will leave me enough daylight to get back to the hut. I would be breaking trail then, so my return would be easier, following my own tracks.

At noon, I stopped and ate some cheese and bread. And looked at the map and checked my Global Positioning System. And listened to the weather radio again. There was no mention of the girl. Does that mean she has been found?

Alive? I was impatient with the dry commentary on air fronts, temperatures, the next several hours' forecast, and ski conditions.

Then it came on. Authorities held little hope for her survival, but the search continued, with more searchers. A special team of troops skilled in cold weather combat had been flown in from Fort Lewis. Are they all stumbling over each other in the same area, I wondered, assuming she hasn't gone more than a mile or two? Or where are they searching? The certainly weren't here. But why should they be? Why would she have raced in a straight line to the east, rather than wandering in a circle, then sitting down to cry, and to freeze to death overnight? Maybe I am the one who has it all wrong. Well, I am just skiing today, and will return to the hut this afternoon, and when and if she is found alive or dead, I can remember that I did what I could, but it wasn't the right place or time. And tomorrow, I will go down from the hut to my car, and go back to Kirkland, and watch the news for the heartbreaking story of the little girl who was finally found. Her parents will be beside themselves with grief, and her classmates will receive special counseling at school, and there will be a photo in the local paper of her empty desk with flowers on it, and children in tears hugging each other.

But what can I do? At two o'clock, it was time to turn around. I don't know what kept me going. Maybe it was the map. And I kept seeing Mt. Katahdin and the Wassatquoik River superimposed on it. Are the angels making me see this? And I knew that I was not going to stop. If I go much farther, I will have to sleep here, then I can make a quick trip to the hut in the morning, I have my thermal blanket; I can easily survive the night. But I am almost where she could conceivably be. Then I had feelings of foolishness, helplessness. Professionals who know the area, the military, and trained, experienced volunteers are searching for her, in a well-orchestrated operation. Who am I?

And then an angel told me to get up and go, and where to go.

CHAPTER SEVEN ────────────────

FROM THE HOSPITAL, THEY TOOK me by van to the County jail in Bellingham. They took away my cell phone, along with everything else in my backpack and my pockets. I had to use the public phone that is made available to detainees. I phoned my attorney in Seattle, and gave him the story in the little time I was allowed. He explained that criminal law was not his specialty, and as the venue was too far away, he wouldn't be able to represent me. "I have my practice to run here." He would have someone in Bellingham contact me. My lawyer was washing his hands of me. He was sending me to the Yellow Pages. He was only the first of a succession of business associates, relatives and friends who walked away quickly.

First days were in a holding tank. Most of the others looked like over-aged street kids; they couldn't give up their skateboards and moved into a lifestyle that had no responsibilities and none but brief rewards. Some were fishermen just back from Alaska who had gotten in trouble with their big paychecks. And some looked as though they had been born there, and would die there. I was out of place. My hair was short, and I had no tattoos nor body piercing. But no one was interested in me, and I was glad of that.

The next day I appeared in a courtroom. The Superior Court Commissioner told me that I was charged with first-degree kidnapping. I was told my rights, and asked if I could afford an attorney. I was still waiting to hear from mine. My bail was set at $25,000.

Later that day, the attorney referred by my mine came to see me. She explained that the charge of first-degree child molestation was to be added.

She had just learned this. I would be back in front of the Commissioner tomorrow morning, to be told this formally. I should expect the bail to be doubled.

Finally, there was someone I could talk to. "Where do these charges come from? Does Miss Noll claim she has been kidnapped and molested?" I was shouting, outraged.

"The kidnapping charge was brought by the parents. The child was in your custody, without the knowledge and consent of the parents. You moved her from the place you met her, to another place.

The molestation charge seems to have come about this way. When the girl was examined at the hospital, she had recent bruises, some on her legs. The doctor played it safe, and reported it to the Child Protective Services, a state agency, who investigate these things, when there is the suspicion of abuse by a family member. Her parents, of course, were still there. They pointed out to the CPS investigator that the bruises were recent- and the doctor confirmed this - and that they hadn't seen her for four days. So then everything turned to you.

So the Sheriff's Department was brought in on the molestation charge, since the alleged offense, like the kidnapping, took place in an unincorporated area. But the interview with Miss Noll was conducted by the CPS interviewer, as she is a professional, experienced in this type of crime. She is a State employee, but she was working in concert with the Sheriff to do this on behalf of the county.

Another item in the doctor's report was that her hymen had been broken but he couldn't place the timing. There was no evidence of forced sexual intercourse, any physical evidence of trauma to her genitals. But the charge is not that you raped her, that is, with penile penetration, but that you touched her in a sexual manner. This would not necessarily leave any physical evidence."

"Let me get this straight. There is no evidence, so I am guilty?"

"It all comes down to the girl's testimony. The CPS interviewer is saying that you molested the girl."

"That's not possible! It didn't happen! And she wouldn't have said that I did! I need to see her!"

My attorney looked at me as if I were crazy.

"The State of Washington has enacted what are called "child hearsay laws." The child is hidden from cross-examination, and the accused cannot confront him or her. The CPS and law enforcement officials act as proxy for the child, and their testimony is unassailable, when the victim is a child."

"She is not the victim! I am the victim! What about the right to face your accuser? You're the lawyer, but I believe you will find it in the Constitution!"

"Mr. Cross, in the State of Washington, we use the Constitution to wrap fish. And that is the more polite of a couple of metaphors that come to mind."

"So what do we do?"

"To defend against the kidnapping charge, show what happened. How you found the girl. Why you could not return her promptly. Against the molestation charge, we can do nothing."

Is this North Korea? Or where am I? Will I awaken from this nightmare soon?

"So what am I looking at?"

"For each of the charges, sentencing guidelines are 67 to 89 months, probably concurrently. Your only shot is a jury trial, but the jury will have to accept the CPS interviewer's testimony. They can't make their own rules, like asking for the girl's testimony."

"What about my saving her life? Isn't that worth something? Even if I did molest her, which I didn't, by the way!"

"What I am hearing, from the papers and elsewhere, is that there were dozens of searchers out there; you were the one who happened to find her. Any of the others would have gotten her back the same day."

"Bullshit! None of the searchers were anywhere near her! I was the only one! We were so far from the ski area, and the resources, that I couldn't possibly have got her out sooner. If the searchers were there, why didn't they find both of us? We both could have died. And she would have died if I hadn't found her. The searchers never got anywhere near her!"

"Mr. Cross, the Sheriff's Department's Search and Rescue people were out there. They were assisted by skilled, experienced volunteers. The prosecutor works hand-in-hand with the Sheriff's Department every day. Their kids go to school together. They are very pissed off that a non-local guy, from Seattle, no less, and an amateur, accomplished what they failed to do. The prosecutor will look for their testimony to counter yours, and they will not treat you kindly."

Yes, this really is North Korea, I thought. *And I'm not going to wake up.*

If only I hadn't turned on the weather radio, I thought. Then immediately, I hated myself for thinking that. If I hadn't turned it on, Missy would be dead. They will do what they will to me, but I won't kill Missy in my mind.

"So I'm convicted now, by a collection of liars."

"There is an alternative. If you admit guilt, you can be sentenced under the Special Sexual Offenders Sentencing Alternative. This means that you will serve only six months, in county jail, and then undergo community-based treatment. But you do have to admit guilt."

Now I felt as though I were at the bottom of a deep well, trying to look up to find sunshine. I could not have thought that such an injustice could be possible, at least not in the United States of America. I thought of the movies and books of the genre of the innocent, or even not so innocent, American caught up in the grotesque and barbaric legal system of a banana republic or other authoritarian state. I thought of *Midnight Express*. But in America? The best alternative I am offered is having my life trashed, losing my family, my home, my reputation, my business, and being marked forever publicly as an admitted sex offender?

I remembered receiving a circular from the Kirkland police, with the photo of a convicted and now paroled sex offender, giving his block address, name and photo, and detailing his crime. "An informed public is a safer public," it said. So Jason's and Franklin's school friends will have a picture of their daddy posted on their refrigerator door. "Look out for this man in the picture," they will be told. "Tell your teacher or a policeman if he tries to talk to you." The circular said that there were thirty-four registered sex offenders living in Kirkland. It didn't say how many paroled murderers there were, or how many convicted of manslaughter, or assault, leaving victims in wheelchairs for the rest of their lives. It didn't say how many convicted extortionists, arsonists, armed robbers, or burglars. Or drunken drivers convicted of vehicular homicide. "Boys and girls, be careful when you walk or ride your bike past that house," the circular should say. "The woman who lives there killed someone with her car, and she is likely to kill again. And at that house over there…" The police wanted us to watch out for, and defend our children against a pathetic-looking sixty-year-old man who had been convicted of having consensually but improperly touched a fifteen year-old girl, and who was found to have dirty pictures in his house.

"That's not an alternative. I didn't do it."

"Then you will have to serve the whole term, with maybe one-fourth time off for good behavior."

"Where?"

"Monroe State Reformatory. It has a special unit for sex offenders. They cannot be placed with the general prison population, for reasons you understand."

What motivates this evil? The state has paid for Monroe, so there is a mandate to fill it, like a hotel needs to fill rooms, a hospital needs to fill beds? Does each city, county, state agency have a quota, like cops for speeding tickets? Or does the CPS get a finder's fee for the delivery of each live body?

I was arraigned on both charges. I got some money from my company funds, and the attorney got a bail bondsman to post bail for me. The trial date would be set within ninety days.

"If you are found guilty, you will be sentenced and incarcerated immediately. So use this time before the trial to put your affairs in order. " The right to a speedy trial is a Constitutional guarantee, I remembered.

I returned to Kirkland. I arranged with my lawyer to proceed with the sale of the business, upon my conviction. He would be ready, but it was going to happen. It would be a distress sale; most of the value was in the name, and it would be attached to mine, now disgraced.

My wife, who had always believed that I could do nothing right, accepted the corollary; if I were accused of doing something wrong, I must have done it. So she initiated the divorce, and her attorney talked to mine. She would get the house, the cars, and most of the savings. She would get something from the sale of the business. Most of this was ok with me, as I would have no way of supporting the children from Monroe. I would be left with enough to cover my legal fees, not much else.

I thought about cashing out everything, and leaving the country. They hadn't pulled my passport. I guess they believed that no American can possibly survive outside the United States, unless under the protection of the military, or as a US corporate employee. I can move easily and alone in many countries, I knew. It was a real option. Would they put Interpol on me? No, I've got to make the record clear, and claw my way back.

After my wife and boys left, I had time to clear out the house. As I was putting things into a storage bin that was parked at the curb, a neighbor woman walked by with her dog, and said, almost gaily, as though she were commenting on the sunny weather, "You're not welcome around here any more, you know!" I think that she was the mother of one of my boys' classmates.

So it's starting already. The police circular wouldn't be around for a few years. I told her that she was on the wrong end of the leash.

"My husband will take care of you!" she sputtered.

I didn't know how long I could pay for the monthly storage of furniture, other big items. So I had made a small collection of things I wanted to keep forever; these went into the storage bin for fifty dollars a month, which I prepaid for five years. The rest, mostly furniture and appliances, were to go to an estate sale upon my conviction. Everything would be gone, when the house was sold. I thought that most men and women heading for prison don't have these concerns; they probably travel lightly, as I did when I was twenty-one, when everything I owned fit in the trunk of my car.

I wondered. Shouldn't the Department of Corrections offer moving consultant services? Stop delivering the paper and disconnect the phone - I'm going to prison. Should I instruct the Postal Service to forward my mail to Monroe? What's the mailing address? I don't have a cell number yet. Does the IRS expect a return from me next year? Will credit card renewals be sent to the prison? They always ask for an activation call from your home phone, for authentication. Is a call from a pay phone in prison ok? Not that I will need credit cards. And the Christmas card list? I heard a loud scratching sound as our names were deleted from lists all over the world.

Even before the foregone conclusion of the conviction, I had been betrayed by nearly everyone I knew. But what they were working with was the obvious, incontestable evidence. The newspapers, the court actions. No one wanted to retry me in their minds. After my wife's abrupt departure with the boys, all family friends went into silence. My few relatives had simply gone quiet. So everyone had cut and run, or simply vanished, without comment, or goodbye. But what would one say, anyway? "Sorry to learn that you have the hots for little girls, and got caught!"? Or, "Keep in touch, and we'll do lunch when you get out?"? Maybe Hallmark should have a card for the occasion.

But for the one champion betrayer, the girl whose life I had saved at the risk of losing mine, and who then accused me with her massive lie, I could feel no enmity at all. Because I knew that she didn't say it.

I was pronounced guilty of both charges, and was sentenced to sixty months on each, to run concurrently.

The two cars were sold, so after I locked up the house, I took a taxi to Monroe to surrender. I took the few things that the lawyer said I would be able to keep. There wasn't much, mostly some books and pictures of my boys.

CHAPTER EIGHT ———————————

IN THE EXERCISE YARD, I was approached by a couple of guys who wanted to talk. I was starting to learn the rules. There were lots of them, according to a book I had borrowed from the Kirkland library, something like "*So You're Going to Prison!*" The rules were, not to be rude to anyone, but don't let anyone step on you, either. Don't be too friendly, or people will take advantage of you. Don't be standoffish either, or you will have no allies.

Don't gamble. Don't lend money or things, and don't borrow. Obey the rules. Be courteous to the guards, but not friendly, or everyone will think you're an informer. Don't be a smartass, to anyone. Lots of rules to remember, but most of them common sense.

These guys seemed ok; they just wanted to see what the new prisoner was all about. They wanted to know what I was in for. I clammed up on that. But I was sure they already knew. Then they started telling me about Monroe.

"It's not as bad as you might have heard, and it's not nearly as bad as other places. Sure, you've got bad stuff going on. But if you're careful, you can avoid it." Rape was what worried me most, but I wasn't going to ask. But they got around to it. "There's not much of that here, at least nonconsensual. The gays pretty much keep to themselves, and stick together for defense."

"What you have to look out for is Fulwood and his gang." One guy nodded toward a bunch of blacks, with their apparent chief, a medium-sized but heavily muscled guy at their center. They saw me glance at them, and Fulwood fixed me with a stare. "There are two real badasses in this prison, and he's one. The other is Lincoln…Abe Lincoln," he smiled; "yeah, that's his real name. But Abe doesn't bother anyone. Everyone wants to see them duke it out. Abe teaches a boxing workout, and he's pretty good. Fulwood wants to go to Fist City with him, to show that he's the big man here. Abe won't fight him. He told Fulwood to his face, in front of his people, that he would kill him if they fought, and he didn't want to spend the rest of his life here. So Fulwood goes around to Abe's boxing workout to taunt him. And Abe takes off his headgear, and holds out gloves to Fulwood, but he won't take them. So it's a standoff. But if there ever is a fight, everyone will be betting. The odds now look pretty even. But they don't fight.

Fulwood's gang is what I started to talk about. They do gang rapes, usually on new guys. That's what you have to look out for. Fulwood doesn't join in; he does one-on-one. So don't ever put yourself in a situation where you are alone. The gang can get you, or Fulwood alone will get you. And there's nothing you can do about it, unless you brought an Uzi with you."

Suddenly, the excitement of being in a new home, with new friends, and new experiences, was starting to fade.

*　　　　*　　　　*

We were having dinner at home, with spaghetti with marinara sauce, sausages, and broccoli, the boys' favorites. I had laid out a wedge of stilton and crackers as a special treat.

"What's *that?*" Franklin asked, looking at the stilton with disdain.

"It's blue cheese."

They loved their parmesan cheese grated on pasta. "Make it snow, Dad!" And Daddy's macaroni and cheese, heavy with a crust of extra sharp cheddar.

But *that?* "Why is it blue?"

"Well, it's a kind of mold."

"*Mold!*" they shrieked, and did pratfalls from their chairs.

"OK, guys," I said when they were back in their seats, "it's more properly called culture.'"

"And I say it's *mold!*" responded Jason. They refused to touch it.

A few nights later, we sat at a booth in a Japanese restaurant in Kirkland. I was in a reverie over the funky wall drawings and calligraphy, and hot sake. My wife was working on a bowl of hot noodles. The boys were having their favorite sushi, a neat rectangle of egg omelet on top, instead of fish, and their loved miso soup. They ate it every time we enjoyed Japanese food out, and I often served it at home.

"Dad," said Jason in a tone that I had learned would precede a difficult question, "What is miso soup made of?"

"Miso," I replied. There was a long pause.

"And *what* is miso?"

"Fermented soybeans," I said, uneasily.

Now both were eyeing me with suspicion. "What does 'fermented' mean?" he asked, drawing the words out slowly. I tried to change the subject, but it was too late. I was trapped.

"Well," I said lamely, "it's like, well, mold."

"Aaaaaaaaaaah!" they screamed in unison, and did synchronized back slides under the table. They wouldn't come up until the green tea ice cream was served.

They wouldn't let it go. Weeks later, as we were leaving an exhibition at the Seattle Cultural Center, Jason wanted to know, "Shouldn't they call it the 'Seattle Mold Center'?"

But Franklin was the funniest. He would, without signal, jump up from the dinner table, do a whooping war dance around his chair, then sit down, deadpanned, and resume his meal as though the ritual were as routine as saying grace.

Or at bath time, after the boys had stripped in their bedroom and headed for the hot bath I was running, Franklin would frame himself in the door, and do a full frontal shimmy to announce his entrance. Jason would observe his behavior with a look of benign amusement, as if thinking, "I was like that, once."

*   *   *

I laughed softly to myself, as I remembered these things.

"You ok, man?" It was Abe, my new cellmate.

"Just thinking of my boys."

"Those guys?" he said, pointing to the two framed photos. "They're good-looking kids." As I didn't know him yet, I felt uncomfortable with this observation, given the inclinations of most of the residents here.

"Thank you," I said, simply. I needn't have worried. Abe Lincoln was a tall, spare black man. He had been convicted of having had sex with his stepdaughter. He didn't deny it; no one in Monroe denied anything, because there was no believing listener. The guilty ones were willing to believe that we were all the same. "I don't want to hear your bullshit story of innocence," was the general attitude. "If you didn't do it, why are you here?"

But as I didn't do it, I was open to the possibility that Abe didn't do it, either; I came to believe this more strongly as I came to know him better. He later simply allowed that the allegations came out of a divorce case "She wanted to have something to beat me with."

"So are you going to join my boxing workout?" he asked.

"Why should I?"

"You might want to hit someone some time. Or keep someone from hitting you. Or them," pointing toward my boys' pictures.

"Are you going to attend my electronics classes?"

"Man, I can't read that shit. I looked at those books!" he said, pointing to the stack on my end of our common table.

"I'll make you a deal. You don't hit me too hard, and I won't give you the hard stuff at first."

"Man, you don't understand! I'm not good at reading, at *all*!" he said, the only time I ever saw him with even a hint of helplessness.

"So, let's work on that. What else have you got to do for the next couple of years? I'll help."

"Ok. It's a deal. But I need to tell you something else." He paused. "I don't know how much you know about things here. You got to be careful. Do you know about Fulwood?"

"Yes. A couple of guys told me about him."

"What did they say?"

"That there are two tough guys here, you and Fulwood. Fulwood is the one to worry about. He likes to rape new guys, like me."

"They got it right. You got to watch out. He'll set you up. You're in special danger because he sees you as under my protection. He'll use you to get to me. So be careful."

Well, I got my exercise, and Abe got his English and electronics. He enrolled in a remedial English class, but it wasn't enough. I had him work on a vocabulary book, first. He'd be up late, reading and writing. I learned to sleep with his light on, and his whispering to himself. There was some synergy working here, because his boxing workouts left me ready for a deep sleep every night. I worked in some electronics vocabulary. We had only four guys in the electronics class, and they were better at English than was Abe. Abe was all smart, but his schools had to have been bad or none. Are we still doing this to our children? I thought angrily, and often. I resolved to make him my personal jailhouse project.

Abe had plans for me, also. "You got the body and the basic strength and the speed," he said, "but you need the moves, and the coordination, and the conditioning. And you need some weight training, too. I'm going to make you into a dancer, Hamlin, a badass fearsome dancer!"

It was great aerobic exercise. I looked forward to the daily workouts. Abe gave me special, personal instruction. I measured my progress against the others in the workout when sparring, and I found myself getting pretty good. Except when I sparred with Abe or Hernandez.

One day, after the others had left, Abe wanted to talk. "Boxing is a sport. There are rules. It's a good way to defend yourself, or beat someone up. But remember that it is a sport. In a real situation, you don't have rules, for them or you. Anything goes. So you need to learn other stuff, like below the belt." And he showed me how to develop a fast and strong snap kick. "You don't want to extend your leg, because he can grab it. So you just snap hard and fast, and get your foot back right away. There is not a better way to take a guy out."

He had me practice this a lot, for speed and power, but not when anyone else was in the gym, or watching. He took a black marker, and put an X on the grimy body bag. "Hit a moving target!" he would shout, as he hugged the bag from behind and moved it to evade my kicks. "Come on, dance!" And he insisted that I make that part of my workout, too. And then with weights strapped to my ankles. When no one else was there.

After Abe had gotten through basic electricity and electronics, two large workbooks, I started him on alarm installation. I would be going back to what I knew when I left prison, and I wanted to have someone like a family member as my first key employee. I didn't know anyone else. All my professional contacts were gone. I had to hit the ground running when I got out.

I started a poetry appreciation class, as an adjunct to the remedial English class that I taught as a substitute. I used the *One Hundred and One Famous Poems* as a basis, plus some Edward Lear, Ogden Nash, even Shel Silverstein, to keep it light. But the class most enjoyed the heavy stuff, like Coleridge's "Kubla Khan" and Poe. Except for a couple of dorks who attended only for credit, I had a good and appreciative audience.

One day, I was on a tear. "Who are the people who wrote these things? Look at their faces!" I shouted, passing around *One Hundred and One Famous Poems*, with photos and daguerreotypes of the authors. "Do you know how they lived? No dry cleaning! No dentists! No real medicine! Horrible hygiene! They were toothless at forty, and dead by forty-five! Yet they were able to rise above their misery and squalor, and write this beautiful stuff that still excites us! Think of that! You want a love story that is common to all ages – read

'Maud Muller'!" And I read it. "Doesn't this make you remember yourself, and someone else, at some time and place?"

Abe said later, "I've never seen you like that before, man. You were possessed!"

"Abe, that's what it's all about! These people were humans like us, who saw through their hard lives these beautiful visions, and were able to record them so that their poems have lived for a couple hundred years. They speak to us across the centuries! And the reason that these poems are still published, and that we are reading them today, is that they are written about *our* lives! Good art, Abe, sticks around for a long time!"

"I never bought that 'old dead white men' shit anyway," said Abe. I noticed that he had more library books stacked up on his corner of the table.

So our respective self-improvement programs moved forward as we worked our way down the long road to release.

*   *   *

One day, I had a visitor. It was Lee.

"Sherry says that you didn't do it." He said this as though he had come here to share with me a piece of secret information, that only he and Sherry were privy to. "She didn't make a big deal out of it, she just said that you didn't do it, period. I don't think that you did, and I'm a pretty good judge of people, but she always gets things right about people. I guess that's why she's so good at selling houses."

CHAPTER NINE ─────────

In San Antonio, I had taken an introductory course in judo, as I needed a sport. I had wrestled in high school, and judo seemed like a natural extension. I followed up with more instruction and workouts, and I made the university team. As in my wrestling, it was win one, lose one. My studies were more important. But I had fastened on the strangulation techniques; my long arms gave me an advantage. I worked on these techniques, and they became my specialty. .

When I left Texas after graduation, I went to Japan early in the summer, to get acquainted before studies began in the fall. The first year was intensive Japanese language study, nothing else. It was necessary to bring the foreign students up to the level to which we could attend lectures in Japanese along with the Japanese students, in the second year. Because it was truly intense, with loads of homework each day, and an exam each morning on the previous day's assignment, the director of the program told us from the start that there would be no extracurricular activities in the first year, no side jobs, no sports, social life, nothing. "You won't have the time!" And the director was right.

But in late summer after I arrived and before school started, after I had found a small apartment and had settled in, I spent time at the campus. I talked to the other students as they arrived, both Japanese and foreign. I was chatting with some Japanese students, as we sat on the grass mound between the administration building and the church and dining hall; they wanted to ask about this foreign student's life, out of politeness, and real interest. During our conversation, I let it out that I had practiced judo in Texas. One of the guys took an inordinate interest in this. There was a reason.

He approached me later, and explained that he was the captain of the school judo team. He wanted me to join. I explained that the rules for foreign students would not let me practice after school started, but I'd be happy to practice during the next couple weeks. "Ok, let's do that," he said. But he had something else in mind.

This is what he was planning: International Christian University was a small school, only 1,600 students. It could not hope to compete successfully against normal-sized universities or even the 10,000-plus student high schools, much less the powerful company teams. But the Mitaka City Annual Judo Tournament was something they faced each year. As tiny as our school was, it was a university, and we had to make a showing. Since the school's organization shortly after the end of the war, we had not taken home a single individual trophy, much less a team victory.

There was a ranking system in each country, but not transferable. I had a black belt awarded through competition in the U.S., but nothing here. That meant that I would compete as a beginner, a non-black belt. I would dominate that category, and bring honors to our school. That was the idea.

The school had a single athletic coach. It couldn't afford more; he was spread out over all the sports. The judo team captain asked him to represent the team with him, in a supplication to the director of our program, to let me join the team, and practice two afternoons a week only, and to participate in the Mitaka City Annual Judo Tournament. That's all. The director apparently agreed; though the captain didn't give me the details, I guess it was something like, as long as he keeps his grades up, and stops after the tournament.

Our team had a manager. She was a second-year student, and was responsible for maintaining records, handling the little finances that were necessary, and keeping everyone on time. She had a hairdo that looked like a mushroom on top of her head. Whenever I think of her, I think of the pretty face capped by a mushroom, and her clipboard and pen, all attention to whatever was going on. She was strict and requiring, and she made no mistakes.

Our team were all sharp black belts, and they gave me some good practice. Nearly all were smaller than I; I was glad to have the experience of guys with fast and clean techniques. I had fought some good opponents in the U.S., but they were mostly big and muscular. These guys were pure judo. This is the country where it was invented, after all. But we all knew that in the tournament, we were up against juggernauts.

In sport judo, you have four ways of winning. The first is a clean throw that puts your opponent decisively on the mat, hard. The second is immobilization, like pinning in wrestling, but you have to hold it for half a minute. Third, a painful arm lock that causes the opponent to surrender. Fourth, and my chosen specialty, strangulation.

Strangulation is accomplished by using the bare arms, or more often, the opponent's collar, to close on his cardioid arteries, causing cessation of blood flow to the brain. The result is unconsciousness. The win is scored when the referee determines that he is out, or much more frequently, when the opponent realizes he is going to dreamland, and "taps out" by signaling a surrender. Sometimes, the referee will mandate a surrender, when he sees the loser's eyes roll up as he passes out. It's like a TKO. The referee must be attentive: sometimes the combatants are so wrapped up in themselves and their clothing that the loser cannot signal. A few seconds of outage is ok; after that, there can be brain damage. We have all been there. The sensation upon waking up is, where am I? Then it gradually comes back.

This technique is well-known to police all over the world. The Japanese call it "shimewaza," or "closing technique." The same verb is used to describe tying a necktie, or the action of a hangman's knot.

In Texas, my opponents knew that to go to the mat with me would be to invite my long, skinny arms to whip around their throats for a quick nighty-night. So they tried to keep me on my feet for a more conventional throw. And often they were successful. But I kept this special skill for when I saw an opening.

The day of the tournament came.

It was in the Mitaka City Recreation Hall, a multi-function arena, with basketball hoops at either end. Wrestling mats covered the center of the floor. The competition among the two classes, non-ranked and black belt, was taking place simultaneously. I saw an elderly man sitting quietly at the side, with his small table with several blank scrolls on it, and his big brush pen and ink tablet. He would be inscribing the names of the winners, for presentation by the head judge. I intended to take one of those scrolls back to the university.

My first three matches were easy. They really were beginners, though two of them were almost my size, and had strength and speed. The fourth gave me a good fight, but I scored with a good, clean throw.

The competition was delayed for a while, so that the final matches of both categories would be for everyone's attention. The final round started with the non-ranked competitors.

My draw was a surprisingly large guy, for a Japanese. He represented Fuji Heavy Industries, which had a factory next to our university. I hadn't seen him in the competition, as I was watching and cheering our team, all black belts. I weighed 170 pounds, and he had easily fifty pounds on me. He looked confident. This foreign kid is going to be a light lunch for me, he seemed to be thinking.

As the match started, I understood what he was. He was eying my legs. No judo guy does that. He's a wrestler, and has just taken up judo. That's why he is wearing a beginner's white belt. But in judo, you can't use a wrestling takedown. It's against the rules. If you are on the mat, it's because of a failed, or half- point throw. You can't just go to the mat. There was a lot of grasping of clothing and positioning, as is usual. But he wants me on the mat. I'm not going to go; I'm not stupid. I can win with a clean throw; he doesn't have the technique. Then he was leaning over, his belt and jacket loose, and that's when I snapped one hand under his collar, the other on his lapel, high, and closed on his throat. Effecting a winning strangulation technique while standing is not usual. But I had him. He was gone. I felt the referee's slap on my shoulder, to signal my win.

Wrong. "Beginners may not use strangulation techniques! Stop!"

And we both retired to the side of the mat, tidied our jackets and retied our belts, and heard again "Begin!"

This time I knew it had to be a clean throw. And he was afraid, and kept pushing me with stiff arms, as beginners do. I slipped low and tipped him over on the mat, for a clean, one-point throw. Or so I thought. "Half-point!" cried the referee. And I had gone to the mat with him to solidify the force of the throw. And when I heard half-point, I knew I was dead. The steamroller was on my chest. It took a full half-minute for the driver to find the reverse gear. And it was all over. He won a full point for pinning me. I lost.

We went back to the campus as the team had done for decades, without a single scroll.

We got in three taxis, and went to a small restaurant on a quiet, shady street near the school, that had a seating area outside in the back. It was autumn, and the leaves on the maple trees all around were in bright colors, and the branches of ginko trees hovered over our table. On one side was a small bamboo grove. There was a bubbling stream fed by an electric pump. A cool breeze blew across us, and we all relaxed after a tough day. We sat at one big table. Our manager ordered several bottles of beer, and some dried fish and seaweed- wrapped rice crackers.

When our glasses were filled, our captain made a short speech. It was about how well everyone did. But we could have done even better, he added. And we must begin our efforts in practicing with renewed vigor, in preparation for next year. In the Japanese way, he did not mention my "but for" win. I was glad. We had all, including our captain, fought hard, and had done our best.

When the speech was over, we were all just talking, drinking a little beer in the fading afternoon light. My reward for the day was hearing our manager, her face lightly flushed from her tiny glass of beer, look at me across the table and say, "Hamlin, you got him as a python snares a wild pig!"

It was only a private opinion, but everyone else knew it, and the school would be talking about how Hamlin, but for a rule and a decision not in our favor, had defeated the big guy from Fuji Heavy Industries. Twice.

As many things were much more important, that day was the last of my judo days. Or so I thought at the time.

*   *   *

When Jason was about five, he asked me an important question.

"Dad, do the good guys always win?"

"No, Jason, they win only when they are stronger, faster and smarter than the bad guys."

"Oh, shoot!"

*   *   *

Fulwood was sitting in his cell, making plans for the evening. The big game was on tonight. He didn't want to miss it. But he had other, more important plans that would take only a few minutes from the game. Maybe he could squeeze it in during halftime? This is the night that he gets to Abe. Enough of this shit. I run this fucking place, and there will be no doubt after tonight. He had had a few words with a guard earlier in the day. It was nearly time for the game. A sudden chill went through the cell. Fulwood shivered. He picked up the prison-issue jacket, and put it on over his t-shirt, leaving it unbuttoned. Then he went to the TV room. The room was colder than usual. But everything was set.

*   *   *

Before my classes were scheduled, I was busy only with my reading and workouts. So I had signed on as a courier, which took me around the prison delivering messages, slips and orders, to offices and workshops, and picking up supplies from the storeroom. It was a plus in the record, to keep busy. But after the classes got going, I resigned. There was not enough time for everything.

But this evening, I got a message from the head guard, saying I was to stand in for someone who was sick. I figured it as someone who wanted to watch the big game. Fill

this list from the storeroom, and then deliver it to the commissary. The storeroom key was taped to it. I was suspicious. This was out of pattern, too late in the day. The commissary was open until nine, but they didn't put in an order like this at night. And it was a small order, quickly made up, I thought. But I didn't want to disobey an order. I couldn't afford trouble.

I didn't want to put this burden on Abe. This was my problem; he had his own Fulwood problem. He wasn't in our cell, anyway; he was at the library or the gym. But on the way to the storeroom, I checked one of the two TV rooms, the one that always had the sports channel on. I saw that Fulwood and his friends were there, commanding the front row, watching the game preliminaries. So I continued to the storeroom, thinking that no one had seen me.

I was wrong.

The storeroom door locks when closed, and can be opened only from inside, or outside with a key. I was standing on a stool, picking orders from the boxes on steel shelves. I had just finished putting the few items in the cart, and was ready to step down, when I heard a noise behind me. I hadn't heard anyone come in. I turned and saw Fulwood. I should have known he would have a key.

"What's up, pretty boy?"

I said nothing. I thought about a weapon. There was nothing but the box in my hand with a pair of cheap sport shoes in it.

"You want to do this the easy way, or the hard way, cunt?"

As he stepped closer, I hit him as hard as I could on the left side of his head with the box. It didn't even get his attention. I jumped down, trying to grab the metal stool, and he hit me. My back was against the shelves as he hit me right and left; all I could do was to protect my head. He was powerful. He slammed me with body punches, and I felt myself going down. Then he put his big head in my gut, while his hands went for my pants. I guess he wanted me conscious; it was more fun that way. And through the fog of pain, I heard an angel shout, "Hamlin! He's wearing a judo *gi!*"

And I saw my manager with her black hair spread like a mushroom, and the clipboard in her hand, with her pen poised to record the score, and my teammates on either side, all screaming for my victory over the big guy from Fuji Heavy Industries, to take the first scroll ever, back to our school.

"As a python snares a wild pig," she had said.

So as Fulwood pushed my pants to my knees and tried to turn me around, I shot my right hand, palm up, under his collar, behind his neck, and whipped my left to grab his left lapel high. I closed my forearms like pliers on his huge neck, all within a second. All my upper body strength was behind this.

My brain screamed: I don't care how much muscle you have in your neck, you big shit! Your arteries cannot hide from me, and I am going to kill you! I ground my wrists into the places where I knew his arteries were lodged. And even if no one else in this world was with me, my manager and my captain and my teammates from years ago, in Mitaka City, Japan were screaming for my victory. This is not your day, Mr. Fulwood, because today the referee is God! You don't know Him, but He knows you! And He doesn't like you! He gasped something about his mother as he realized what was happening, and swung both of us to the floor. I kept my death grip on his throat, and my left elbow hit hard on the concrete slab as we crashed. I thought it was broken. But I wouldn't let go. Then he was on top of me and trying to hammer my head, but my grip kept his ugly face close to mine. There was nothing he could do. Then his eyes swam up and out of sight, and he collapsed. I managed to roll him partly to my side; my pants were around my knees, so I couldn't get on top for more leverage. But I would not give up my grip. I knew that three minutes was about the limit; the brain approaches death after that. So we lay there like two lovers, while I thought.

I didn't want a dead man in the storeroom; I decided that I wanted to leave something that would have just enough brain cells to let him play patty-cake with his therapist. There would be no more muggings, no more fights, no more rapes. There would be TV and videos; he could watch tonight's game over and over for the rest of his life and not know who was playing, much less the score. And except for maybe a baby's pacifier, there would be no more entertainment than that for Mr. Fulwood, for the rest of his godless life.

And I thought of this as one way I could repay the State of Washington. Take care of my child, Governor; change his diapers twice a day for the next forty years, and think of me each time you go to the pail.

These thoughts flashed quickly before me, but then an angel shouted "FULL POINT!" and I released my grip. I pulled my hands away from his collar, and turned him to lie face up. I knew it would be a few seconds before he became conscious. I pulled up and straightened my clothes, then grabbed the metal stool. I stood behind his head.

After a while, his eyes opened. He stirred. He couldn't see me. There was only a disembodied voice.

"Don't move. You're in the storeroom, and still alive. But if you move, you will have this stool sunk in your head, for good. I can kill you, and I can get away with it. I should be here, and you shouldn't. But I don't want to kill you."

There was a long interval, as he slowly came to understand the events of the past few minutes.

"What do you want?"

"I want you to listen. One. The rapes stop. You, and your friends too. You control them. Two. You make peace with Abe. You two hang together and keep the others straight. Three. You join my poetry appreciation class. Do you agree?"

"And if I don't?"

"You're dead, now. Now. Or, maybe only a head injury that will leave you goofy for the rest of your life. You're stronger than I am, but I'm faster, and I'm in control now. And I'm a good person, Mr. Fulwood. God is on my side."

He waited.

"What if I lie to you to get out of this?"

"Will you?"

There was a long pause. "No. But let me talk to Abe, alone. Don't make me look bad."

"Ok. No one will know what happened here, unless you tell them. I won't. I'll talk to Abe, too. He can be trusted. But one other thing - you make it clear to your people that nothing – I mean nothing - happened here."

Abe was in our cell when I returned. He was seated at his chair at the end of our table, reading. I sat down in my chair, at my end. I pushed my chair back, and took some deep breaths. Then I told him the whole story. "I don't think that either of us has to worry about Fulwood again," I said. Abe just sat there quietly and looked at me. Then I stood, went to the toilet, and threw up.

That night, as I lay thinking about how I would have to hide the bruises— maybe skip showers for a few days and just wash out of the sink—and wondering if my bruised and blackening elbow were broken, I thought about what had happened, from start to finish. Fulwood had set me up, with the help of the guards. But I also knew that an angel had visited the prison. No one wore any top but our green/brown t-shirt inside; the jacket was for the exercise yard, on cold days. Fulwood was the only one I had seen wearing this today. I couldn't have defeated him had he been wearing only his t-shirt. The angel was also coaching me from the side of the mat; she showed me how to beat him, and then saved him from my inflicting a lifelong injury on him. I gave her, the referee angel, a special prayer of thanks for this, for saving both of us from my rage.

For the first time since I had entered prison, I knew that I wasn't alone anymore.

I didn't want Abe to hear me cry. I'm twenty-six, right? So I could only leak tears, face-down into my prison pillow as I thought of the clean beauty of the snow on Mt. Baker and the shining of the sun on the mountain, and of a beautiful child with red curls who smiled at me with pure love and hugged me, and of my sons. And these thoughts lifted me above the darkness and dirt that I lived with. I said a prayer of gratitude to God and his angels whom He sends to help me when I need them, and who give me the inspiration and strength to defeat these infamous creatures from hell.

Good to his word, Fulwood talked to Abe and they shook hands. "We're walking on the good side now, Fulwood." To this day, what I did to Fulwood is known only to him, Abe and me. And when there was a big game on, sometimes Abe and I would join Fulwood in the sports TV room, in the front row. And in the next couple of weeks, I had new enrollees in my electronics and poetry appreciation classes.

Besides Fulwood, there were two each from his old gang. They couldn't figure out what I had done to him. He had walked into the storeroom with his usual intent, and had walked out a changed man. They knew I was a good boxer but not *that* good, so it had to have been electronics or poetry. And they were determined to find out for sure which, and exactly how it worked.

Fulwood's gang had a new leader from the ranks, but briefly. Until he was found with multiple facial bruises, then resigned from the position. And then they were all in English class, or cabinetmaking class, or auto body repair, or in my beginning electronics class, or poetry appreciation. The Fulwood gang was no more.

One Sunday morning in chapel, Fulwood came in and sat on the seat to my right; Abe was on my left. After the services, he turned and squeezed, then hit, my upper arm, and walked out, without a word.

CHAPTER TEN ——————————

MY JOB WAS TO AWAKEN the boys; my wife would then take over to dress them and make them presentable for school, while I fixed their breakfast.

I would open the blinds and announce, "Boys! It's a sunny-bunny day!" Or rainy-painy, or cloudy-dowdy or foggy-doggy. Whatever the conditions. Daddy the cornball weatherman.

Jason, on the upper bunk, would stir, and open his eyes just enough to fix me with a look that said, "I'm sleeping. How can I get you to understand that?"

But Franklin would roll out, grab a bolster longer than he was tall, shoulder it and go after me. "Oh no! Help!" I would cry as he whacked me again and again.

I had read somewhere that compulsive rhyming is one symptom of a mental illness. Well, nobody's completely healthy. But Franklin had the definitive statement on the subject. One time I was urging him to eat something, and I told him, "Franklin, it's yummy in the tummy!"

"Daddy, I don't want you to say that to me any more."

"But why, Franklin?"

"Because I'm almost five!"

If I don't have the joy of these memories to sustain me, I am dead.

*   *   *

There was a big snow, and my two elder brothers took me to the big hill just beyond Jimmy Glover's house. They brought our two sleds. All the kids were there; it was the biggest hill in Salem. I was only five, and my brothers left me alone while they sledded. After a while, I knew that they weren't going to share, and I started crying.

Some big girls had a toboggan, and one ran over to me and hugged and kissed me so that I would stop crying. Then one of them put me on the toboggan with the other girls, and we rode endless times, it seemed, and I was surrounded by love, as each time a different girl would wrap her arms and legs around me and hug and kiss me. There were happy screams and the snow swirling around us, and the cold bite of the wind in our faces as we raced down the hill.

And when it was time to go home, two of the girls took me by the hand to the top of the hill, and delivered me to my brothers, who waited, sleds standing up next to them. They looked at me with surprise and envy.

Well, guys, either you have it or you don't.

And that afternoon's experience lodged in my mind forever; except by Mom or Dad or Grandmother, I had never been hugged or kissed. There were so many girls who loved me, and competed to hold and hug me. And my little heart overflowed with joy on that day. I learned about new dimensions of love, and of the sheer sensuality of those pretty, apple-cheeked faces rubbing and kissing mine.

It was a small town, and the girls were upperclasswomen at PS 1 where my brothers went; the girls were about ten or twelve, I guess. I wasn't even in school yet, but I got more Valentine's Day cards than either of my brothers did.

And now I'm in prison because I helped a Big Girl, saving her from the snow and ice that would have killed her.

You go figure.

*   *   *

My younger brother died on his birthday, when he was taken off the respirator. I took a four-cell Maglite from his cabin, when we were taking his things away. I kept it for a long time, and now and then turned it on to reaffirm his life; they were still his batteries. And when I saw the brilliance of the light, I remembered the smart little guy with his insolent ways, that I went camping with and fought with, and the big mountain man and cowboy that he was when he died. I wasn't sure what I would do when his batteries went, so I didn't check it very often. But that was before prison. I don't know where the flashlight is now.

But even a big mountain man is no match for a pickup truck filled with construction tools moving at sixty miles per hour. And so the last time we were together was when I spotted a grove of aspens on the side of a mountain that he loved to hike; the angels had arranged them in an almost perfect circle, to receive him. And that's where I placed his ashes.

*   *   *

Missy was always hovering in my thoughts; she was a collection of intense and beautiful images, my last pleasant experiences. These clear and sweet thoughts, in juxtaposition with the reality of my days and nights in prison, were painful to deal with. But they wouldn't go away. The little girl, her sweetness, her innocence, her strength and her loving hugs and smiles were always just below the surface of my thoughts. And sometimes broke through.

One evening, I was lying on my bunk looking for patterns in the ceiling. Abe was whispering over his books and writing things. Someone was playing a collection of songs by the Highwaymen - heavy with guitar, and the voices of the country and western greats.

An image floated across my mind. It was Missy, when I took my last snapshot, outside the hut, just before we descended the mountain. She was playing in the snow as I locked the hut and got ready. She saw the camera. She cocked a hip, put her thumbs in her ears, waggled her fingers and stuck out her tongue.

At the same time the refrain from one song came into the cell–

> "When this old world blows asunder
> And all the stars fall from the sky
> Remember that someone really loves you
> We'll live forever, you and I..."

Remarkable timing, guys. And I was glad that I had the top bunk, so that Abe couldn't see my face.

Then I sat up sharply. The camera! What happened to it? Was it confiscated as evidence? I hadn't noticed that it was missing when I was released from jail, and got my backpack and its contents back. I had too many other things to think about. But where were the camera and film?

*　　　　*　　　　*

One evening we were returning from somewhere, and I turned in the driveway, stopped, and got the boys out. Jason said, "Look, there's a cat!" And I looked, and saw a black cat with a huge white spot on its front, limping across the street that we had just passed through. Did we hit the cat? Is that why it is limping? I was sure I hadn't. Maybe someone else did.

The cat entered the driveway, and approached us. I couldn't see well. We opened the front door as the porch lights came on. The cat was there, expecting to come in with us. I sat down on the front step, picked up the cat to see its injury. It was a three-legged cat, missing its left front leg. There was a clean heal; it was not a recent accident, maybe it had been born that way. But it wasn't an it; it was a she, and pregnant.

I know about cats. Don't take them in, or they will never go away. I closed the door carefully. The cat has a home. Not here. But the cat wouldn't go away. It was mewing very softly. My experience with stray cats is that they would project their voices to the extent that they would be sure to reach the one softhearted person in the house, so as to gain entry or at least milk. They evolved that way.

But this three-legged, pregnant lady was simply whimpering quietly.

My heart gave in. I brought the cat inside. My wife and a lady friend agreed that she was indeed pregnant. What to do? I tried putting her outside again. She wouldn't leave our doorstep.

We brought the cat back in. But how do you care for a cat? Especially a pregnant cat? I had no experience. We made her a bed, and I went to the market and got some cat food, and litter. I had no idea how much of each to buy how long will she be with us? Then I was hit with a jarring thought –hey, slowpoke, pregnant means kittens!! When?? And what do we do?

We talked it over. We have to find its home. I called the police department, to see if there was a lost cat report. Nothing. I thought about posters. I will need photos before I go to the print shop. Tomorrow I will talk to neighbors. Someone must know about this cat; with only three legs, and her ungainly swinging belly, she could not have come far. But maybe someone from another neighborhood dumped her? There are people who do things like that.

The next morning, after I had taken the boys to school, I started walking the neighborhood, going first in the direction the cat was coming from when I first saw her. Then I saw a moving van in front of a house in the next block. So far, so good, Sherlock! But how to approach these people? So you thought you could simply leave, abandoning your crippled cat, great with child? Think again! Do you know about the SPCA? And that they have police powers?

I went to the door, rang the bell, and waited. A busy housewife, with dust cloths and stuff waving all around her, came to the door. I told her about the cat, and that I wanted to return her.

"We don't have a cat. But what does it look like?"

"It has three legs only, and is very pregnant. It's not your cat?"

"Oh, that's 'Polky'! "Polky lives next door!" she said, pointing. "And it's a he, not a she! He's just fat!"

"Has three legs?"

"Yes, she said he lost a leg when he was a kitten, an accident."

"Ok, I have the cat at my home, so I'll bring him over to her."

"She's not home during the day, so you might try later, around six."

So I left a note on the door of Polky's mistress, with our home phone number.

That evening, a woman called, and asked if it were true that we had her cat. I said yes. May I bring him over? Please do!

Since the boys were involved in the rescue effort, they wanted to come with me. And I carried Polky back home. I rang the bell. A thirty-ish woman came to the door, and looked at us as though we were a team of cat thieves. She nearly snatched Polky from my arms. She was bristling with hostility. I explained how we came to have her cat; the cat appeared to be injured, pregnant, would not leave our doorstep, was crying pitiably, and we assumed it had been abandoned.

"Abandoned?" She held the cat up for all of us to see its glossy coat and healthful condition. She looked at me as though we were returning it only because of a fit of conscience. "He would have come back by himself!" But for you, was the insinuation. "Thank you so much for your concern!" The last word was delivered as an ice cube spit from her mouth.

So we don't help abandoned, crippled, pregnant cats, and we shouldn't try to help twelve year-old girls dying on a cold mountain. I just keep getting things wrong. She would have found her way back to San Diego by herself.

*   *   *

Brooke was a French horn player in our junior high school orchestra. I was in love with her. I would look at her as we practiced. She was more important than the notes I was playing, even though I was first-chair in the trombone section. When I looked at her, I would miss notes. On the day after the last day of school, I went to the band room to get my trombone to take home.

Brooke was there too, and we were alone for a moment, as she got her French horn down from the shelf. She smiled at me. Then we sat on two folding metal chairs, and started a bashful "What are you going to do this summer?" conversation. Brooke told me that her father was being transferred to Argentina, so she would not be back in the fall. They were leaving soon.

I told her what I knew about the angels. That they keep a notebook on everyone, recording the good deeds, and bad things like not tidying up your room, or not turning in homework assignments on time. "Or missing notes!" Brooke laughed. But they don't record really serious stuff, the things that get in the newspapers. The angels are pure and innocent, and God has other agents who take care of those things.

The most serious transgression that an angel can record, I told Brooke, is to really like someone, and not to tell that person. This is so bad, that the angel cries when she puts the entry in the book.

"Brooke, you may laugh at me, or slap my face, or throw up. But I don't want angel tears in my notebook, so I will tell you now that I……love you."

Brooke stood up, and I stood up. She wrapped her arms around me, and we hugged. And we kissed each other, once.

Then Brooke said, "Goodbye, Hamlin", and before she turned away to pick up her French horn and leave the room, I saw that her eyes were wet.

As she left, Mr. Holtzman, the orchestra director, came in the door. He saw Brooke's teary face, and then saw his first-chair trombonist weeping in the corner. He quickly left the room.

I never saw nor heard from Brooke again.

*   *   *

When I was twenty-one and in my last year of college in San Antonio, I often had breakfast in a diner near school, sitting at the counter. I was attracted to a very pretty waitress who was, I later found out, twenty-nine. Linda was the star among the waitresses; the others were pleasant but ordinary-looking. Linda enjoyed or endured, endless, mostly innocent, flirting remarks from the students, repairmen, salesmen, plumbers and bankers at the mostly-men, nearly always-full counter. She got a half dozen marriage proposals a day while pouring coffee, and most of them could have been in earnest had the proposers been single, and had some money. They knew that she undoubtedly had a husband or a boyfriend, anyway.

Linda knew to never ask any of the guys, "Is there anything else I can do for you?" or "Is there anything else you need?" But it was all good-natured banter, and they threw occasional, similar remarks to the older, stouter waitresses too, to keep everyone happy.

Occasionally there was the proposal given in a low voice, which fact signaled a serious attempt; she always deflected these with face-saving humor and grace.

I didn't join in any of this, but I noticed that I got a direct look and a real smile each time she stood in front of me, and there was more eye contact and more touching than was needed to place my oatmeal and dish of fruit in front of me. I knew to hold my coffee cup when she came with a refill, because she put her hand gently on the cup also as if to steady it, which meant her fingers were on top of mine briefly. She didn't do this to the other coffee cups, I noticed.

I was new at this. I couldn't ask her for her phone number, or give her mine, in front of everyone. Or maybe I was imagining all this. That's how they get good tips! Or maybe I remind her of her kid brother? Then I had an inspiration. I thought -- I know how to give her my phone number without arousing any suspicion, and without embarrassing myself if I'm mistaken.

I had a part-time job, commission only, selling legal plans, like prepaid dental plans, to anyone at the U who would listen for a while. I made a little money from this. I had cards with the company logo on them, and my name as Independent Associate, and my own phone number. So the next time she poured my coffee, I made a joke about pouring it on me, so I could sue the diner. "I need the money for school!" She and a couple of neighbors laughed, as they recounted the famous real incident along these lines, the lady who got hot coffee in her crotch and sued. Then I said, "Really, if you do spill coffee, or even biscuits and gravy on someone, and you need a lawyer, here's where to call." And I handed her my card, looking at her straight. She understood.

She laughed, her eyes dancing. The neighbors didn't have a clue. "Thanks! I'll keep this! I might need it!"

She didn't call. I didn't know what her schedule was, as I was there only in the morning. Most of a week passed. That Sunday morning, the phone rang. I knew the diner was closed. I hoped it was she. It was. "Good morning! This is Linda! What are you doing today?"

It was early, and I guess my voice was froggy. I thought for a second. I usually took a walk by the river, the Riverwalk promenade, and had coffee and a newspaper, and thought that this would be a safe way to get acquainted rather than suggesting a dinner and movie. I was still inexperienced and klutzy with women, like Dustin Hoffman in *The Graduate*.

I replied, "Umm, take a walk."

She hung up. NO!! I don't believe this! I didn't have the chance to say, "Will you join me?" Maybe my inflection was wrong! At any rate, she was gone. There was no way to reach her today. All day, I suffered. I knew that she was crying from shame at being put down, that she had misjudged. He was just trying to sell me a lawyer plan, that's all, jerk!

The next morning I went to the diner as usual. She wouldn't look at me, and wasn't joking with anyone. She looked as though she would break into tears any minute. One of the other waitresses took my order. What should I do? I can't approach her here. But where? Then I had an idea. I opened my book bag, took out a small piece of paper, and wrote a short note. And when I left and went to the cashier, I borrowed a stapler, folded the note and fastened it. Then I found the elderly manager and told him, "Sir, I'm afraid I was really rude to one of your waitresses, and I didn't mean to be. Could you please give her this note?"

"Sure. Which one?"

"The lady with short black hair, standing at the counter now, pouring coffee."

"Oh, Linda! Sure, I'll give it to her. I wish all our customers were as polite as you are, son."

I stayed away from the diner. She didn't call. For two weeks. I was miserable. She had called me; she had made it clear that she wanted to see me. And I screwed up. But I explained in the note the misunderstanding. Why wouldn't she accept that? Why wouldn't she call? Maybe I just don't understand women. I don't get a second chance, that's it. She thinks that it's an apology, and hey, I've got plenty of guys who want me, and I chose you, and you rejected and humiliated me. I'm not a beggar. Or…maybe the manager didn't give her the note. Did he recognize an old and often-tried trick? How many times have customers tried to pass notes to Linda?

I had to know. I went back to the diner, for what I resolved to be the last time.

When I came through the door and she saw me, Linda nearly jumped. She couldn't hide her happiness, and I think everyone at the counter saw it, and were surprised and envious; her joy spilled out all over her face. This tall skinny kid with a book bag must be her kid brother, come for a surprise visit, they thought. She didn't even take my order, but stood in front of me and said.

"You gave me that lawyer's card, and I lost it, and I want to call him." Linda paused for a moment as she thought of a subterfuge. "I'm having trouble with my neighbor and his dog, and I want to call him."

"Oh, I think I have another one of his cards," I said as I pretended to rummage through my book bag. "Sure, here it is!"

All the guys all started to chime in with legal advice about neighbors and dogs. And I sat there like a dummy decorating a counter stool. She got the note! But she had thrown away my card, and that's why she didn't call, idiot! She couldn't! And you're a university student? Go back to grade school before you do more damage!

Then she took my order. And served it. She could have served me cow pies on a bed of gravel, for all I noticed. I had been hauled up from the pits of misery to the peaks of joy. And when we did the coffee cup thing again, she gave me a radiant smile, full of huge promise that went straight into my heart and lodged there.

When she called, I enunciated slowly, "I plan to take a walk this morning along the Riverwalk. Would you like to come with me?"

"Love to!" she laughed.

It was a short walk. But it turned out to be a long day. Because after we sat for a while by the river and had toasted bagels with raisins inside and cream cheese on top, and coffee, Linda took me to her apartment. That day she taught me a great deal. About misunderstandings. And how, when they are straightened out, sometimes they can be astonishingly rewarding.

Chapter Eleven ———————————————

AFTER THREE YEARS, I WAS released, just after my first parole hearing. My record was good. I would have to register as a level-one sex offender, the lowest level, one seen as not likely to re-offend. But it was explained to me that in Washington, there was the "two strikes, you're out," law which provides for life imprisonment without chance of parole for the second sexual offense against a minor.

Well, I didn't do the first one. Will someone identify me, and out of malice or fear, accuse me a second time? Can I stay in this state? Can I stay in this country? The law didn't permit me to defend myself against the first accusation. Should I bet the rest of my life that it will permit me to defend myself if there is a second time?

But now, I needed a job. I still had my electrical contractor's license; there apparently was no provision in the law to take that away from me just because I was a felon. But I didn't have the capital to start up my company again, and was facing a new city. It's hard enough to break into the business as a clean newcomer, much less an ex-con on parole. I had kept up my membership in the Washington Burglar and Fire Alarm Association, using my lawyer's address. I guess they wondered who this guy was; he never attended the lunch meetings of the Bellingham Chapter.

I attended the first lunch after my release. I kept quiet, feeling out what was going on, and was afraid someone would find out from where I had just surfaced. But no one asked. There was a lot of discussion at the lunch about the shortage of qualified alarm installers, and marketing people. And the constant issue of false alarms. I felt as though I had never been away.

Felix was sitting next to me. He was quiet, and seemed to be mystified by everything. While we ate our lunch between speakers, he confided that his brother and sister-in-law had owned and managed Whatcom Home Security; it was their livelihood, and their lives. They had a couple of commissioned sales people, and his brother also did sales, and installations, while his sister-in-law handled the office, the phones and the books. They had a full-time installer who had just quit. The timing was especially bad, because Felix's brother had just died. That's why he was here.

Felix needed someone, urgently. He couldn't just leave things with the grieving widow. He had taken over the company. But he needed someone who was experienced, and had a license; the company had had one, but the administrator's certificate, without which the license is worthless, had died with his brother. I had both. And so there was a match, and I was on the payroll the next day. Felix knew little about the business, but was doing his best. He was retired, and so had the time. He gave up his daily golf game, and wouldn't let anyone forget it.

I checked out the equipment. They had two white vans, with ladders on top, and orange cones on the bumpers, lettered Whatcom Home Security on the sides and back. The alarm systems were ones I was familiar with. After spending a few hours with Freida, I saw that their back office procedures were standard, and looked carefully professional.

Things worked out ok. I took over the installations, and worked on a good marketing plan. And then Abe got his release.

Felix gave me a long stare when I brought it up. "I can't put two convicted sex offenders on the payroll! That's not a quota requirement!"

I suggested gently that that would be part of the deal. We needed another person, and I knew and had trained Abe. "Think of it this way, Felix: It will be your USP."

"My what?"

"Your Unique Selling Proposition. You get not one, but two perverts installing an alarm system in your home. Just be sure to get the kids out of the house first."

Abe came to work, and went on installations with me, and after a while he was ok on his own. Felix, Frieda, Abe and I were doing just fine.

I rented a one-bedroom apartment overlooking Bellingham Bay. It was a bit expensive, but I was earning well. The old skills were coming back; I hadn't missed much. I was really driving the place, and getting a good hourly rate plus commissions on deals that I originated. I was putting away money, and after a while, put a down payment on a piece of land on the Nooksack River; it was a private deal, since my credit record no longer existed. I planned to build a cabin, to have a vacation place for the boys when they visited.

My book collection was gone, so I spent some weekend time at a couple of book exchange stores, reconstructing my small library. So during the first year of parole, the work, jogs by the bay and reading filled my time. Abe was teaching boxing again, this time at a Boys And Girls Club. I would join him a couple times a week, in the evening after the kids' hours, for a workout. Sometimes the older kids would be in the later workout, and I was often challenged. But even at my advanced age, I gave as good as I got.

The past was gone, and nothing to think about. My boys were the only link to my previous life, and they visited nearly every school holiday. Everything else was gone. I knew I would be in Bellingham forever, even after parole ended. Mt. Baker and its glacier, and its snowy slopes, and the Nooksack River fed by the glacier, was where I wanted to be.

In those days, I had no female company, and I wasn't really looking. There wasn't a vacuum to be filled. My idea of a romantic evening was to sit at the Lone Star bar and listen to Patsy Cline sing "Sweet Dreams," while I nursed a bottle of beer.

For a while, I dated a girl from the local university, Western Washington University. Judith was a political history teaching assistant, and the organizer of a prisoners' advocacy group. She was pretty, articulate and pleasant, but after a while I got the feeling that she was more interested in me as a former prisoner than as a partner. I didn't want to rehash that part of my life. So we had a few mediocre meals and not very interesting conversation, and that pretty well sums up our relationship. I did, out of courtesy, attend a meeting of her advocacy group, where Judith introduced me to Ray Plotkin.

Ray was a criminal defense lawyer, in private practice in Bellingham. He was a small, intense man, all serious, and as bright as a supernova. He wanted to know about me. For some reason, I didn't mind telling him the story. Then I understood that he already knew the story, and was just nodding at the places where I filled in the details. It was big news four years ago; I just hadn't had access to newspapers then.

Judith told me later that Ray was doing a lot of pro bono work. He was so often at the courthouse with prisoners who didn't have any money, that she wondered how he survived. He was really an unpaid public defender. The students who were involved in the group, and other activist groups, worshipped him. "He gets results," Judith said. "A few years ago, he got an innocent verdict for a man who shot a policeman dead, in front of ten witnesses!"

I had to wonder about that one.

"Anyway, he doesn't lunch or golf with the local Bar Association."

I started spending some time with Ray. I wanted the convictions reversed. I wanted my record cleared. We were both looking for ideas.

CHAPTER TWELVE ─────────────

I'D BEEN WORKING HARD ON a proposal, a business alarm and surveillance configuration that was taxing my knowledge and experience. It was important to close this deal. I was responsible for my own deal originations, which meant lots of door-knocking, and anything else we could do to bring in business. Felix had said "I didn't hire you as an installer!" Back to the proposal. I tore up a sheet of schematics, and started over. There was a knock on the door. It was after midnight. I wasn't expecting anyone, and didn't want a surprise visitor, now. I opened the door.

It was Missy.

Her hair was no longer red, it was light brown, still curls, but short. She wore glasses. She was taller, still slim. No braces showed as she gave me a tentative smile. The look was partly relief at, I later learned, having ended a long, difficult journey, and trepidation – is he going to hit me?

I didn't move. What? I thought. Why is she here? Then I saw that she looked really worn and tired, and was standing up a big backpack with her left hand. "Come in?" I said.

We both sat down at my small kitchen and dining table. She took off her glasses, and looked across the table at me. Tears filled her eyes, and rolled down her face. "Hamlin, I *never* said anything bad about you!"

I fixed some coffee. We talked for much of the night.

"After I left the hospital, they took me to a place, that I found out later was the Child Protective Services, part of the state Department of Social and Health Services. My mom went with me. She said that the nurse wanted to talk to me about what happened on the mountain to make sure that I was really ok.

The nurse started out by asking where I had been hurt, why these bruises. I told her that they were caused because I fell down on my skis, and later, when I was on your back, we fell a few times, but weren't hurt much. Then she asked about when we were sleeping together. She asked me if you touched me. I said that my toes were frozen, and you rubbed them so that I wouldn't get frostbite. And you warmed my feet. 'Where else did he rub you?' 'On my back, when I was really cold and shivering.' 'Where else?' 'My ears, and hands, I guess.' She asked me if we had washed; I told her you fixed me a sponge bath, but you waited outside. She asked what we were wearing in bed, and I told her. She asked if you took off my panties. I got mad. I stopped talking. She went to a cabinet, and took down a girl doll. It was naked, but shaded in the crotch and breasts.

She told me to show where you had touched me. I pointed to the doll's toes, and ears, and hands, and back. 'And he didn't touch you anywhere else?' 'NO!' I shouted. I had been to the classes in grade school, where the school nurse told us what our mommies had told us, that there were ok places for adults to touch, and bad places, where nobody touches except mommy or a doctor or nurse. Then she asked me if you had kissed me. 'Yes,' I said. 'Where?' she asked. I pointed to my forehead, and my right cheek. 'Show me on the doll,' she said. I pointed to those places. She said, 'But you already showed me all the places he touched you! You didn't point to those places! Where *else* did he touch you?' '*No place!*' I shouted.

'Sarah, you lied to me once. Are you lying to me now?' Then she said that you had admitted to the police that you had touched me there. 'He did not touch me in any bad place!' I said. 'Sarah, I am very patient. I will wait here until you tell the truth. If you don't stop lying, you will be taken to a hospital for a while, until you remember. We want to protect you from him. You just have to tell the truth,' she said. 'I *am* telling the truth!' I screamed.

There was a fat policeman in the room, too. She said he was there to protect me from you.

The nurse left the room, and came back with my mother. 'She refuses to cooperate,' she said. My mom leaned close and said, 'You tell the nurse the truth, and do it now!' The nurse said, 'Show me where he touched you,' pushing the doll in front of me. I grabbed the doll and threw it in her face. My mother slapped me and I was crying, really hysterical.

The nurse said 'It's all right. I have what I need. She admits that he kissed her, that they were clothed inappropriately, and that he bathed her, and touched her. She changed her story about where he touched her. It's pretty clear that she's in denial. I've seen this before.'

My parents took me back to San Diego, and said to forget all about what happened. I couldn't forget. I asked about you, and my mother said that if I kept asking, that I would be reported as a sex offender, and the San Diego police and my school would be notified. Can you believe it? My own mother? I was only twelve!

Anyway, I guess I tried to forget, and hoped that you were ok. I had no way of knowing. But I knew that someday I had to get out of that house, with those horrible people. So I just moved along, doing the right things. I wouldn't let them destroy me.

I wasn't like the other kids."

I noted the "wasn't." She had burned bridges.

"I wasn't into dating, mall shopping and stuff. I was invited to try out for the cheerleader squad! Can you believe anything so brainless?"

"So what did you do?"

"Studied hard. Read books, lots of history. Track. Tennis. I was captain of the debating team. We beat other schools. I guess everyone thought I was a first-class nerd, but the guys were always after me. I have one boy friend, not boyfriend, nothing romantic. Arthur. He is a genius, not just with computers. He was at our house a lot. He taught me a lot. He is also a champion pistol shot, and he gave me lessons at a range, with .22 caliber pistols. The broker didn't like him, because he wasn't a jock."

The broker?, I wondered.

"My other friend is Claire. We are all three friends, and we were always at each other's houses. We all had other friends, of course, but the three of us were especially close.

One day about three weeks ago, when I came home from school, my mom handed me a ski magazine that had come in the mail. It had a printed mailing label addressed to me. 'Since when do you subscribe to a ski magazine?' she demanded.

'I don't,' I said.

'Then why is it addressed to you?'

'I don't know. Maybe it's a free sample. I didn't order it,' I said.

'Well, don't even think about it,' she said. 'You and your skiing have caused enough trouble in this house.' But she didn't take it away from me. I went to my room, and just tossed the magazine on my bed.

Later that evening, I was taking a milk break from my studying, and was sitting on my bed, listening to Leann Rimes. I picked up the magazine. It was a special issue on rescues, avalanches and lost skiers and stuff. And I read something in the editor's column. And I stopped for a couple of seconds, and I screamed! My mom came to my room, but I always keep the door locked, so I had time to hide the magazine. I told her I was napping and had a nightmare or some excuse, and she left. I looked in the mirror. My face was white.

Well, this is what I found. Missy handed me a wrinkled magazine column, with several lines highlighted.

"Better leave the rescuing of children to the professionals, or at least the experienced with credentials, or have plenty of witnesses. One guy in Western Washington found this out to his regret, when he "rescued" a twelve-year-old girl, then took her to his mountain hideout for a few days. He was charged with and convicted of child abduction and child molestation, and went to the slammer for his adventure."

I got on the phone to Arthur, and told him what I needed to do. He told me to get on our phone connection on the net, so that no one could listen in on us. Arthur knew how to get anything, anywhere, and by early morning we had all I needed. I knew you were out on parole. The divorce was there. Your address. Everything.

The next day, I didn't go to school. Neither did Arthur. We'd both been up all night. Nobody made the connection. But I wasn't sleeping, I was making plans.

I borrowed money from some of my girlfriends, and from Arthur. I took all I had saved, too. I had about nine hundred dollars in cash. I told my friends separately that I planned to go to San Francisco next week, and not to tell *anyone*. Well, I knew that someone would blab, and it wouldn't be Arthur or Claire, and it worked. I was traveling light, only a book bag, so no one would think I wasn't a commuting student. But by the time the school and my parents heard San Francisco, I had been there and gone.

I knew that they could trace me through bus drivers as far as San Francisco; that's why I didn't try to leave a fake trail to another city.

But when I got there, I contacted Claire's friends in Berkeley, college kids, and they put me up. We did a complete disguise. Look! I dyed my hair, and cut it short. I had brought some fake glasses left from a school play. I even put on a temporary tattoo, a snake around my neck! I had to be careful when I showered!" She laughed. "And I got these clothes from the free table at a shelter for street kids. Not exactly Donna Karan, is it?"

She still had dressed stylishly. Missy would look good dressing out of a Dumpster, I thought.

"I don't know if they were looking, but I know that they didn't find me. After a couple days, I got on Amtrak and headed for Seattle. Before I left, I stamped and addressed and postdated a bunch of postcards from San Francisco, to my girlfriends. And the kids sent these out according to the dates. I was keeping in touch with Arthur, and his friends passed me on to some friends in the University District. He had told me that I could always reach him by e-mail. 'Just find an Internet cafe,' he said. 'Don't risk a phone call.' But his friends were all wired, so it was ok. From there, it was a matter of being passed off to their friends in Bellingham, at WWU. The funny thing is that no one asked me where I was going, what I was planning to do, but they all helped me. I had some trouble with the guys who are always at bus and train stations looking for runaway girls to put to work, but I was careful. And now, here I am."

"But why didn't you contact me?"

"Because all you knew about me was that I must have testified against you. I was afraid I wouldn't be welcome. I had to come directly to you, to explain. I knew that your wife had divorced you, and figured that you were doing some nothing job somewhere here, because of your record, and being on parole."

"Well, I lost my business in Kirkland, of course. But I'm doing ok."

"But why did they put you in prison? You saved my life! And you didn't do anything wrong!"

"Your parents made a big thing about your being away for four days. They made such a big noise about it, that the police got in on it, and the prosecutor's office was notified, and I was arrested. They didn't contest the fact that I had saved your life. But they went on to claim that I thought that I had the right to keep you as a pet for a few days. They didn't accept my explanation about the weather. They said there was no reason we couldn't have gotten down from the mountain right away, or found the searchers. They had some hotshot ski patrol guy who said it would have been a piece of cake. But they weren't facing what we were facing; your skis were lost, and I was not an experienced skier. They said that you had your own skis, that you wouldn't have delayed me. They wouldn't believe that your skis were lost. They laughed. How do you lose a pair of skis? They suggested that I had thrown away your skis so that we could stay in the hut. They kept calling it a 'lodge,' like it had a roaring fire and a gourmet kitchen. Of course, you were not there to support anything I said.

And your testimony, or what they said was your testimony, was enough to put me away. They wouldn't let me or my attorney talk to you even if you had still been around, or even give us a transcript of your interview. The interviewer simply testified that you had said that we had slept together, with no pants on, and I had touched you, and that you had lied and changed your story several times about where I had touched you. That I had given you a bath. And the interviewer said that this supported a charge of molestation, and the court did not challenge this testimony. That was enough. The law in Washington let them get away with this.

Actually, I could have been sentenced to forty years. But the judge took into account the fact that there were unusual circumstances, I had a clean record, a family man and so on. But when sentencing came, I was told that I could avoid prison, just six months' jail, by admitting guilt. I would then have to undergo community-based treatment. But I told them that I had done nothing wrong and didn't need treatment. I didn't make any points in the courtroom by telling the judge that I thought that he needed treatment.

So there I was. I won't tell you about the years in prison. It's all over.

Now, Missy, we have to plan. Are you willing to retract–or correct–your testimony?"

"That's why I'm here, Hamlin! In three weeks, I'll be eighteen, and they can't shut me up. And I won't be a runaway!"

"I'm going to talk to my lawyer first thing tomorrow. But it's important that you stay hidden for the time being. At some point, they might give up on the San Francisco thing, and start looking here, which means me. Are you ok with the people you're staying with?"

"Sure, for now."

"Missy, it's two a.m. I don't want you going out now. I've got a bed and sleeping stuff for you. Stay here till morning, and I'll drive you to your place."

I fixed up the couch for her, and got out towels and things, and a big bathrobe. "Do you need pj's?" "Sure, I'll borrow yours, if it's ok!" she laughed.

She showered and otherwise busied herself in the bathroom. When she was ready, she rushed out and hurriedly started rummaging in her pack.

"I nearly forgot! Hamlin, you must have put your camera in my pack by mistake, on the morning that we left. I found it when we got back. My mom found it in my room, and demanded to know where it came from. I told her. I didn't steal it; it was an accident and I wanted to send it back to you. She got angry, and took it away. But I had already taken the film out. And I knew that she would be looking for the film, so I had put it inside one of my dolls and she never found it. And later, I developed the film. Most of the shots weren't so good, but I chose the best one and blew it up." She pulled out a rolled and wrinkled 5" x 6" color photo of us, sitting behind the small table in the hut, draped in our blankets, and sitting close. I don't photograph well, but Missy made me look good. We were both smiling happily, as Missy made rabbit ears behind my head. "Anyway, I still have all the negatives," she said, placing an old envelope on the table.

As I lay awake for a while thinking about what had happened in the past few hours, I thought that things could be good again, really good again. Missy had come back.

The angels had shown her the way back.

*   *   *

We had a breakfast of cornflakes with milk, and an orange and coffee.

I called Ray at home early, and told him I had important news; I wanted to see him soon. He was ok for nine.

Instead of taking Missy to her friends' home, I took her to Ray's office, after explaining to her what Ray and I wanted to do.

I introduced Missy to Ray, and told him briefly about the events of the last few hours.

Ray was furious. "You what? You did what? She was in your apartment last night? She is a runaway? Do you know that, number one, you violated parole by being in contact with her, and number two, have contributed to the delinquency of a minor?"

Then I told him the whole story, Missy filling in. Ray settled down.

"Ok! Ok! But last night didn't happen! Both of you understand that?

Here's what we do. Put her in a safe house, where no one can find her, until her eighteenth birthday. No, no. Missy, you stay with Nancy and me. That's it. Sorry guys, but I need to know some things for sure, like where you are, Missy. We will have some protection, like lawyer-client privilege, maybe. I'll need you to sign something. Hamlin, you and Missy do not contact each other except through Nancy or me. Missy, after your birthday, we have a coming-out party, a press conference. Missy tells all. We ask for a retrial based on your testimony, and I will make sure that we are all over the newspapers."

Then I told him of my idea to find an expert on cold-weather survival; we need someone with authority and experience, to beat the kidnapping charge. I knew that there was a Special Forces unit at Ft. Lewis, whose training includes mountain combat. There must be someone there.

"This needs some work, but let's discuss it," he said.

I asked him "Could Nancy show Missy around?"

Ray looked blank for a moment. Around our one room? Then he called, "Nancy, could you and Missy get acquainted, like at the coffee shop across the street? I'll treat for donuts."

After they left, I said to Ray, "We have to talk about payment. You've given me lots of time and help, and you haven't billed me."

He gave me an incredulous look, as if to say, what are you thinking about?

"Hamlin, I like you, I really do. And I know that you are in the right, or I wouldn't be in this. And now that I have met Missy, I have to say that I like both of you, maybe love you guys, really! But Nancy and I are not the Red Cross. We will get a reversal of your convictions. But that's only the necessary first step to a civil suit against the county and the state. The reading that I have so far, and now with Missy's testimony, is that we can go for the gold, and Nancy and I will get a piece of it. That's what's going on, Hamlin. Stick with me, we sink the bastards, and we all win, and we all win big!"

Chapter Thirteen ━━━━━━━━━━

A FEW WEEKS LATER, I met with Ray to go over the trial strategy.

"We are looking for a decision to reverse your two convictions, child kidnapping and child molestation.

The first, we will accomplish with Andrew Ross's testimony. He's completed his survey, his interviews, everything. He does good, careful work. I think that with his credentials and his reputation, his testimony will be unassailable. The locals who presented their flawed testimony five years ago are nothing compared to what Andrew has done. He's had some help from his Army friends at Fort Lewis; and they have assisted him in surveying the site, on skis. No one will challenge the Army!" He gave me a copy of their report, written by the senior of two Special Forces ski instructors.

"On the child molestation charge, we will rely heavily on Missy's testimony, of course. But that's not enough. We want to show that her testimony five years ago was falsified. I don't just want to get you off the hook, I want the court to see that you were convicted on the basis of false testimony. That's why our second witness will be the Child Protective Services person who interviewed her, and who testified as proxy for her."

"Missy said there was a second person in the room, a cop. What about getting him on the stand also?"

Ray gave me a look of, what, you really don't know? Where have you been?

"That was a detective named Graber. Graber usually initiated investigations relating to child abuse crimes, and gave them to the prosecutor. He was behind your case. You should remember him."

He paused for a while. "I didn't tell you about Graber before, because it would have been a distraction. He's not relevant."

"So why not?"

Ray took a deep breath. "Four years ago, he and a CPS interviewer questioned two kids, boy and girl, early teens. In their home, in front of their mother, about alleged sex activity with their father. When the father came home, he was enraged. He went to the station and demanded to see Graber and the CPS woman. He raised hell. They weren't there. Nothing came of it. But they got his number.

These were clean, decent people. They were good, normal kids. They had good grades. She played the flute in the school orchestra. He was on the basketball team. The dad was a league bowler. Mom was a part-time librarian. They were like the families that you used to see in TV sitcoms, not the contemporary crap.

The father was a bit of a redneck, but of the milder variety. He was a telephone lineman, fifteen years on the job, clean record. He had a short fuse, but he'd never been in trouble. This was a good dad. I believe to this day that Graber had received some bad information, probably mistaken identity. But the die was cast.

The next day, the father went bird hunting with his buddies. When he returned home with a couple of ducks, he found his border collie dead on the front lawn. Inside, he found his wife, hysterical, her arm in a sling, in the living room, surrounded by neighbors. There was blood on the carpet.

Graber and a city policewoman had come to the house, and taken the boy and girl to a facility, 'for their protection'. His wife had been roughed up as she tried to protect the kids; they had dislocated one shoulder when they put cuffs on her, and she had just come back from the hospital. And she told him that the boy had been slapped hard by Graber when he took a swing at him, trying to protect his sister. The little border collie had gone for Graber, and he shot her. The wife said that he was to surrender at the police station on child abuse and sexual offence charges. And she was also being charged with interfering with a police officer.

Well, he got in his car, and went after Graber. He found him easily at a coffee shop near the police station, where he hung out with his friends. A witness said that they were all laughing about something when the kids' father walked through the door, blew off the top half of Graber's head, laid his shotgun on a table and sat down. Then he ordered coffee.

I defended him. But anyone could have done it. When I learned that he was being charged with first-degree murder, I nearly peed my pants. 'Murder first' means premeditation. There could not have been. There was no time. If he had gone out and bought a gun, or if he had waited until the next day, the county would have had a case. The prosecutor was new on the job, and knew that he had to win his first big trial. It was a cop killing, right? And in front of witnesses! He had to fry this guy, or be out of a job, forever.

I showed that my client was in a state of uncontrollable rage. His wife had been assaulted and injured defending their children, his kids had been physically attacked and stolen, and his home violated. His dog had been shot dead in his living room. And he was being accused of unspeakable crimes against his son and daughter. Look at his frame of mind. It went directly to the shotgun, still in the trunk of his car, and the easy target of Graber. We didn't plead temporary insanity; we pleaded not guilty to first-degree murder. If the prosecutor had gone for a lesser charge, my guy would still be in prison. In the jury selection, I made sure that it was full of parents. And dog owners. The prosecutor didn't see what I was doing. So the verdict was innocent. No other was possible. He walked. And he made a big show of going down to the police station, and getting his shotgun back. It was a big story, four years ago."

"Sorry I missed it. I was away. But may I ask who the CPS interviewer was?"

"Stop showing off, Hamlin. I already know how smart you are. She was the same one who interviewed Missy. Her name is Nogales."

So Graber was behind my prosecution and conviction, and he knew about the false testimony. Because he was in the room with Missy and Nogales.

I recalled the words of Ambrose Bierce. "There are four degrees of homicide: felonious, excusable, justifiable and praiseworthy..."

Chapter Fourteen ————

DURING THE PROCEEDINGS OF THE second trial, to reverse Hamlin's convictions of kidnapping and molestation, the statement of the Child Protective Services interviewer of six years before, Mrs. Dolores Nogales, was read to the court.

"On this date, I interviewed Miss Sarah Noll, age twelve, at the request of and in his company, Detective Sergeant John Graber of the Whatcom County Sheriff's Department. During the interview, I determined the following: That Mr. Hamlin Cross and Miss Noll had slept together three nights, two of them in his mountain cabin, in a bed intended for one. That they were only partially clothed, with no pants. They had pressed together intimately and kissed. Miss Noll was touched inappropriately on her private body areas. Mr. Cross bathed her on one occasion. Detective Sergeant Graber proceeded to charge Mr. Cross with first- degree child molestation."

*   *   *

Missy was sworn in, and was being questioned by Ray Plotkin for the defense. Missy was back in her navy-blue skirt, white blouse and floppy blue tie. She was ready.

"Miss Noll, during the three days and three nights that you were with Mr. Cross, did he at any time touch you in your genital or breast areas, or view either of these areas of your body?"

"He did not."

"Miss Noll, did you at any time tell Mrs. Nogales or anyone else, that Mr. Cross had touched you in either of these areas, or had seen you unclothed?"

"I did not. I made it clear to her where I had been touched; never in inappropriate places, the ones you described. And I was always clothed in his presence. And he was always clothed in my presence. And we had to sleep in one bed because there was only one bed in the hut, and enough blankets for one person. There was no heat in the hut. We slept together to keep from freezing to death. And we didn't wear our ski pants because they were frozen. They were crusted with ice, like our jackets. I told Mrs. Nogales all that."

"And what was Mrs. Nogales' response?"

"She said that she knew that I was lying. And that if I didn't tell the truth, that I could not return home. She said that Mr. Cross had admitted molesting me; all I had to do is tell the truth. I knew that she was lying, that he would never have said that, and I didn't fall for her trick. She threatened me. She said that I could be sent to a hospital in Idaho where I would stay until I remembered what happened, and tell the truth."

"Was there anyone else in the room?"

"At first there was no one else, but then a short, fat policeman came in; she said that his name was Detective Graber, and he was there to make sure that I was safe. And later, when Mrs. Nogales left the room, he said, 'You're not going to go home until you tell the truth, Sarah.' I'll never forget that. Then she came back with my mother, and they both started threatening me, and my mother told me to tell the nurse what happened, and slapped me. But I still refused to lie. He never touched me. He never did anything wrong. He saved my life on the mountain while everyone else was sitting around doing nothing!"

Missy stopped, her mouth set, and her eyes filled with tears. "He was punished for something that he *did not do!*"

There was quiet in the courtroom as Ray turned his gaze to the jurors for a few moments.

Then, "Thank you, Miss Noll. I have no further questions."

*   *   *

The Deputy Prosecutor, Mr. Perkins, began his questioning: "Miss Noll, you have testified that Mr. Cross did not see you unclothed. Is that correct?"

"It is correct."

"Mrs. Nogales' testimony is that Mr. Cross had given you a bath. Did Mrs. Nogales invent this?"

"Yes, she did. I told her that he had *fixed* me a bath. He did not *give* me a bath."

"I'm sorry, but I do not understand the distinction."

"You do not? Are you not an elementary school graduate, Mr. Perkins? Or perhaps English is your second language?"

Judge: "Miss Noll," he said, rapping the gavel. "Please just answer the question! Without comment, please!"

"I apologize to the court. I am trying to do my best. But I heard a statement of Mr. Perkins' inability to understand simple English words. I did not hear a question."

The judge frowned at Perkins. "Would you like to put a question to the witness, counselor?"

Perkins was red-faced. "So will you please tell me what is the difference between '*giving*' and '*fixing*' a bath?" As soon as he said this, Perkins wished that he were back at home, in bed, his head under the covers.

Missy looked at him with clear contempt. "One *gives* a baby or an invalid a bath. Or *bathes* that person. Or -- one can *fix* or *prepare* a bath for another person to bathe alone. The latter is what Mr. Cross did. He heated some water and put it in the washbasin, gave me a bar of soap and a small towel, and a saucepan with some more warm water. He left the hut, and returned after I finished washing. I was covered when he left, and I was covered when he returned. He shouted at the door before he came in to make sure I was decent. And that is what I told Mrs. Nogales, very clearly."

"And then did Mr. Cross bathe also?"

"I do not know, but he certainly did not bathe in my presence. I saw him throw my bath water outside the door, and then scoop some snow to heat more water for the basin. Then he went outside. I heard him shouting and laughing and singing 'The Drinking Song' from *La Traviata*. When he came into the hut a while later, he said that he had scrubbed himself with snow, as they do in Finland."

The spectators were being entertained today, and they loved it.

"And was he clothed when he came back in?"

Missy stared at him with disgust. "Yes."

"It's remarkable that you have such a facility for recall, after a period of six years, from the age of twelve, Miss Noll. Especially since your recollections are totally at odds with your testimony as recorded at that time by a trained professional."

Missy looked out the window.

"I am waiting for an answer, Miss Noll."

Missy looked at her watch. "I am waiting for a question."

Perkins' face reddened again. "Then I'll try again. Can you account for the discrepancy between your testimony today, and that of six years ago?"

"There is no discrepancy. I was not permitted to testify six years ago. You know that. The court has heard a paragraph of lies composed by another person."

"But Mrs. Nogales has said that these were your statements. Or perhaps you have forgotten?"

Ray was quickly on his feet. "Objection, Your Honor. The court has heard no such statement from Mrs. Nogales."

"Sustained."

"I have forgotten nothing, Mr. Perkins. I testified only a few moments ago as to what happened, and what didn't happen. Or perhaps you have forgotten?"

The gavel rose, then was suspended in mid-air, as if it were a bird in flight floating into a thermal updraft. It lowered slowly and quietly as Missy continued to speak. She turned to address the jury. Her voice was soft, but commanding.

"Mr. Cross and I were the only ones on the mountain, in the hut. Our testimony is consistent. I am a decent and honest person, and I know Mr. Cross to be the same. Neither of us deserves to be slandered by this sewer-brained liar, speaking under the color of authority of the State of Washington."

The judge was frozen. Missy's words were delivered straight from her head and her heart. The jurors had never seen a person like this. The most cynical among them could not deny this powerful and articulate assertion of goodness and truth.

Deputy Prosecutor: "Your Honor, we object to this invective directed toward a witness."

The judge recovered. "Miss Noll, I caution you to moderate your remarks."

Deputy Prosecutor: "The fact remains that the statement of Mrs. Nogales controls here. She has made a statement that was based on an interview with you. She was authorized under State law to testify on your behalf."

"Not any more," Missy sang. "I am eighteen, and am now permitted to testify for myself. Aren't you missing something?"

Judge, wearily: "Please, Miss Noll. You're not a lawyer ...yet!!"

"Are you impugning my integrity, or my intelligence, Mr. Perkins? I am a National Merit Scholar. I have been accepted for admission to Harvard University. I don't think you could be admitted to the Harvard University snack bar. I am not a liar, and I am not a fool!" Her last statement was nearly drowned out, as laughter and applause erupted all over the courtroom. A cry of "You're beautiful!" broke through the clamor.

Objection, Your Honor, thought Ray, leaning back and smiling. The witness is badgering the prosecutor!

The gavel slammed down. "Order!" The judge's shoulders heaved slightly as he stifled a small laugh. He looked uncomfortable, but said nothing. Perkins asked for it, he seemed to be thinking.

Perkins just wanted it to be over, before Missy could draw more of his blood. I'm the junior guy. That's why they gave me this shit job. They knew we couldn't win. I'm going to get a gun. I'm going shoot her, then the prosecutor, and then myself.

"I have no further questions, Your Honor."

Judge:"You may step down, Miss Noll."

Mrs. Dolores Nogales, the Child Protective Services interviewer of six years ago, was sworn in. She was questioned by Ray Plotkin for the defense.

"Mrs. Nogales, do you recall your meeting with Miss Sarah Noll, and your interview with her?"

"I do."

"Have you heard the transcript of that meeting, prepared by you, and over your signature, read in the court in earlier testimony today?"

"I have."

"Is the transcript of that meeting consistent with the interview you had with Miss Noll, your questions and her answers?"

"Yes, it was and is correct."

"You goddamned *liar!*" shouted Missy, standing, her body trembling, her face red with rage.

Now the judge was angry. He rapped his gavel hard. "Miss Noll, an outburst of that sort will not be tolerated in this court! Do you understand? If you are out of order again, you will be removed from the courtroom!" Nancy was quickly on her feet, hugging Missy and whispering something in her ear. Missy nodded. They both sat down. Missy glared savagely at Mrs. Nogales. She was ready to climb over the table and rip the woman into pencil-sized pieces. She wasn't twelve any more.

Judge: "The jury is instructed to disregard Miss Noll's statement." But the jury had received the message, again. This was no act. She's crazy like a fox, the judge thought.

Ray asked, "Mrs. Nogales, did you represent yourself to Miss Noll as a nurse?"

A long pause. "Yes."

"And were you qualified to so describe yourself?"

"No. It was just to gain her confidence. To make her comfortable."

"So you began the interview by lying to her, is that right?"

No answer.

"Please answer my question!"

"I was trying to help her!"

"Answer my question."

"Yes."

"Mrs. Nogales, did you tell Miss Noll that Mr. Cross had admitted molesting her?"

Nogales looked pained. "Yes."

"And were you aware that Mr. Cross had in fact denied molesting Miss Noll?"

No answer.

"Answer my question, please."

"Yes. It is an interviewing technique. The girl was in denial. I had to get through to her."

"An 'interviewing technique'! Is that what they call lies over at the Child Protective Services these days?"

Nogales was silent.

Ray looked at the jury. "Wow. We're barely into the interview, and a grown woman who claims to be a professional, has lied twice – massively - to a twelve year-old girl!

Mrs. Nogales, have you made a recording of the interview available to the court?"

"No."

"May I ask why not?"

"Because it was not recorded."

"But Mr. Perkins has just said that it was recorded. 'By a trained professional,' he said. Did you make that statement to him?"

Mrs. Nogales squirmed. "No."

"Well, why was the interview not recorded?"

"It was not required. It is not part of the procedure."

"Well, perhaps Mr. Perkins meant, not an audio recording, but simply a written record of the questions and answers. Have you made your notes available to the court?"

"I did not take notes."

"So Mr. Perkins has misspoken. There was no recording of Miss Noll's statements, either audio or written, by a so-called 'trained professional' or anyone else! But may I ask why you didn't even take notes?"

"It is not required procedure". Then she snapped: "I don't make procedure, I just follow it!"

"Even though you knew that your report of the meeting would be used as evidence in a criminal court proceeding?"

"That is not my concern. My concern was to determine the truth and protect the child. That is what I do."

"Oh, the truth! You drop the word so casually, as though you are old friends! In fact, Mrs. Nogales, you haven't even been introduced!"

Mrs. Nogales was red-faced, and looked very distressed.

"You have said that you follow procedure, is that right?"

"Yes."

"As established by…?

"The Child Protective Services, of course."

"Is lying to a child part of the procedure?"

Silence.

"You have admitted lying to Miss Noll twice in the interview. I asked you if lying to a child is part of the procedure that you so closely adhere to. Please answer my question."

"It is not procedure."

"So another lie, this time to the court." Ray looked around the courtroom, his gaze resting on the jury. Then he pointed. "Is anyone keeping count of this woman's lies?"

Silence.

"So lying is something that you regard as optional, that you may employ as an 'interviewing technique' as you put it?"

"Sometimes subterfuge is necessary, as in a police interview, to determine the truth, then, yes."

"Oh, so the State lies when interrogating terrorists, chainsaw murderers and sixth-grade girls, to determine the truth! Mrs. Nogales, my mother and my father taught me that a lie is a lie is a lie. But you have 'interviewing techniques', 'to gain someone's confidence', 'to make one comfortable' and now 'subterfuge.' Do you have any more?"

Silence.

"Do you turn your integrity off and on as you wish, Mrs. Nogales, as one would do with a light switch?"

Now Perkins was on his feet. "Objection, Your Honor. He is badgering the witness!"

"Overruled." But then he said quietly to Ray, "Counselor, you're working close to the line."

Nogales was silent.

"Today, which position is the switch on, Mrs. Nogales, truth or lies?"

"I am under oath. There is no reason to prevaricate."

"Good! Another word for a lie! I love working with a person with a thorough knowledge of her subject! And I am glad that you have enough respect for the court that you will not prevaricate today! But what kind of respect did you have for a little girl, whom your profession is charged to protect, who had just undergone a traumatic experience, when you flat-out lied to her, in front of the intimidating presence of a large policeman? You tell me that!"

"Assisting her in recovery from the traumatic experience was the purpose of the interview."

"I am not speaking of the experience for which there is no evidence nor testimony. I am speaking of the real experience of near-death from hypothermia and exhaustion. She had just been released from the hospital. And you took this opportunity, with your policeman friend, to try to bully her into lying, to incriminate an innocent man. To advance both of your miserable careers. And you failed. Because the little girl was stronger than both of you, together. So you simply lied to the court."

"All I wanted to do was to present the truth about what happened."

"Oh, there's that word again! The liar suddenly wished to embrace the truth! You lied twice in the interview with Miss Noll, and you refused to record the interview or to take notes, to cover your lies. And you lied to the court today. Sorry, Mrs. Nogales, but you have no credibility here, today. The report of the interview that the court heard today simply sprang from your imagination. Is that not right, Mrs. Nogales?"

She recited her formula. "It is a statement of what I learned about the encounter from the interview with the girl."

"But, please tell the court, how did you 'learn about this encounter,' as you put it? What was your source of information?"

"The girl, of course. There was no other source."

Ray looked at her hard. "'The girl.' Is that what you just said?"

"Yes." She knew she was in trouble.

The door to the furnace room slammed shut. The huge rat was trapped. The rat that had nourished its body and brain from the sewer, and had given nightmares to the children living in the floors above, for years. Now, Ray the janitor picked up a two-foot length of rebar, and intended to kill this thing.

"Mrs. Nogales, listen to this question carefully. Did Miss Noll tell you that Mr. Cross had touched her in her genital or breast areas, or had viewed either of these areas on her body?"

"She was afraid of him! They slept together, for God's sake, half naked, for three nights! She lied in the interview, kept changing her story!"

Ray paused for a while, as if in introspection. Then he shook his head slowly as he muttered in a low voice, but audible to the jury: "So *Miss Noll* lied!" He paused for a few seconds, and took a deep breath. "Wow!" He then looked at Mrs. Nogales, then at the jury, then back at his witness.

"Mrs. Nogales, may I remind you that you are under oath, and that you are required to answer my questions, and that you are required to answer my questions truthfully and accurately. The court requires this." He paused for a moment. "Now... this question can be answered only by a 'yes' or a 'no,' Mrs. Nogales." He waited five seconds. "Did Miss Noll tell you that Mr. Cross had touched her in her genital or breast areas, or had viewed either of those areas on her body?"

"Let me tell you something. I have a Master's degree in Child Psychology, specializing in forensics, and sixteen years' experience with the Child Protective Services. I am a professional. I've seen this before, many times. She was in denial. She was only twelve! She couldn't face what had happened to her! She had..."

BANG! The judge slammed the gavel down hard. "ANSWER THE QUESTION!" he roared.

Nogales paled, said nothing for a moment, then turned her pleading face to the prosecutors for help. They looked away. Her hopeless gape met the murderous face of Missy, then the cold faces of contempt of the jurors and a hundred spectators.

"No," she said. Her face fell into her hands as she began to weep.

A chorus of epithets of outrage and disgust erupted from the spectators. A young spastic man raised himself unsteadily on his walker and shouted "You goddam bitch!" I couldn't have expressed it better, thought Ray

"Thank you, Mrs. Nogales. That will be all," he said.

Deputy Prosecutor: "We have no questions, Your Honor."

"Stay in your seat, Mrs. Nogales," ordered the judge. He was distracted for a few moments, while he read something. "Bailiff, take Mrs. Nogales into custody under charges of perjury, and obstruction of justice."

"Yes, Your Honor."

But Mrs. Nogales wouldn't leave her seat. There was a problem. The bailiff spoke briefly with the judge, who then announced a recess. The bailiff needed help. The odor first hit the court recorder, then the defense and prosecution tables. The recorder looked up at the judge with pleading eyes, and nodded toward the witness chair. The judge stood and leaned; he saw a widening, dirty puddle around Mrs. Nogales' chair. He ordered the courtroom cleared, and extended the recess until the next day.

Later, I asked Missy what Nancy had whispered to her.

"She said, 'Don't worry. Ray is going to kill her.'"

*   *   *

Andrew Ross had been called as an expert witness for the defense. The question to be resolved was whether Hamlin Cross had acted reasonably in keeping Miss Noll in his company for a total of three days from his finding her, or whether he could have returned her promptly to her parents.

He was sworn in. The first questioner was Ray Plotkin.

"What is your occupation, Mr. Ross?"

"I am a Lieutenant Colonel, retired, US Army."

"Colonel, what was your occupational specialty?"

"I taught and trained survival."

"Could you elaborate on that, sir?"

"Certainly. US forces may be called upon to fight anywhere in the world. They may have to protect themselves against a situation of no support, on their own, in a variety of climactic and weather situations, from desert to arctic conditions, and everything in between. I personally served in combat in freezing conditions in the Korean conflict, and in the semi-tropics of Southeast Asia."

"How did you come to develop this expertise, sir?"

"Well, I started skiing about the time I started walking. I grew up in Colorado, and was skilled in rock climbing and mountain climbing before I was out of high school. I won a few local and national awards in downhill and cross-country skiing.

When I received my Army commission, I was assigned to survival schools, partly because of my interest, and what were seen as my credentials. I trained with the Special Forces, including mountain and ski combat training. I was an observer with NATO forces in northern Europe. Over a period of time, I moved into a position of teaching and training, then advanced beyond the Army's existing body of knowledge, to researching accounts, both contemporary and historic, of what determines whether a person survives or dies. Even the Soviets, their military historians, cooperated with me on this. Much of this research was related to cold-conditions survival. All these experiences were reduced to rules of behavior, which then were embodied in training going forward, and tested in field conditions."

Plotkin: "Your Honor, I move to have the witness qualified as an expert in winter survival."

Judge: "Any objection?"

Perkins: "No objection, Your Honor."

Judge: "The court accepts Colonel Ross's qualifications."

Plotkin: "Col. Ross, have you familiarized yourself with the circumstances and events of March 4 to March 8, 1995, involving Mr. Hamlin Cross and Miss Sarah Noll?"

"Yes, I have."

"And how have you done this?"

"By interviewing both, by reading Mr. Cross's very detailed account of the event, by speaking with the Mt. Baker Ski Patrol, the Whatcom County search and rescue organization, and the Forest Service people in the Mt. Baker District. I also reviewed US Weather Service reports, including advisories, for the area for those days. All of this was against the background of USGS maps of the area of interest. In addition, we had assistance from the Army, in doing an onsite survey. The court has heard their deposition." There was a long pause, and a shuffling of papers.

"Colonel Ross, based on your experience and your knowledge of the incident, do you have an opinion as to whether or not Mr. Cross acted in a reasonable manner in his conduct in recovering Miss Noll from the mountain?"

"To answer your question directly -- yes, I believe that he acted in a reasonable manner. But if I may... I would like to add my opinion that he did an admirable, heroic job. I don't know anyone, with his lack of mountaineering and skiing experience, who could have pulled this off. I am amazed by what this man did. Using the little information that he had, from the weather radio report, his topo map and GPS, he intelligently and deliberately sought and found the girl, miles from where the others were searching. And gave her the nutrition and warmth without which she would have died. But for Mr. Cross, Miss Noll could not possibly have survived the second night. And the next day, against great difficulty and danger, moved her to safety in the hut. I give this man full marks."

"Did he do what you would have done?"

"Initially, yes. I like to think that I could have acted as competently as he did. He was good! He acted prudently up to the point at which he decided to leave the hut on the fourth day, to descend the mountain. That's where I would fault him." There was a stir in the room.

"Sir, do you mean that in your judgment, they should have remained in the hut longer?"

"Yes. They should not have left the hut. That's one of the rules. Stay where you are, as long as you have resources, and you know there will be searchers. He was not a skilled skier. Moving himself around was about the limit of his ability. He went down the mountain carrying an 80-pound weight on his back. The selection of cross-country skis depends partly upon the body weight they are to support. He was a 180-pound man, who suddenly weighed 260 pounds. One serious spill could have finished both of them. They were both bruised, as it was, and exhausted, from numerous spills. And when they couldn't ski, they had to wade through the heavy snowfall of the previous day. The exhaustion could have stopped them, then death by hypothermia. He didn't know that, but the final stretch, from the ridge to the road, had been declared an 'Extreme Danger' zone because of the risk of avalanches.

If they had stayed in the hut, they would have been found within two or three days, at the most. Even if no one was looking for the girl in that area, on the east slopes, the Forest Service knew where he was headed. He had left a flight plan, as usual, at the ranger station, and his family would have reported him missing after a few days. His car was parked at the base of the mountain, at the takeoff point for cross-country skiers and snowshoers on the east slopes. And his friend who owns the hut would have known he was missing, and would have directed the searchers to the hut as an obvious first look. He had a red light flasher on the hut that would have made finding them easy, once a search had begun.

They had sufficient food to be comfortable for two or three more days, and to survive for another week or more. They were running low on fuel for his stove. That was the biggest limiting factor, but they would still have survived. And their morale was good. This is very important. They both had their heads on straight. They had their checkers and their books."

There was another long pause, with much shuffling of papers, and whispers. The prosecutor's boat appeared to be dead in the water. Defense was cutting smartly through the waves in a brisk wind.

"Colonel, we are going to tread on delicate ground here. Mr. Cross and Miss Noll have testified that, after the first night in the snow cave, they slept huddled together in a small bed, each clothed in their upper garments, and underpants only. Mr. Cross has said that they did this to conserve body heat. Is this consistent with your knowledge and experience?"

"Yes. The best way to retain body heat is to put flesh against flesh. Limit the exposure to cold air. That's why you instinctively hug yourself when you're cold. The evidence suggests that the girl was suffering from hypothermia. You can read any popular handbook about skiing or winter camping, about how to deal with hypothermia; you put the victim in a sleeping bag with another person, or two, with little or no clothing between them. Ok? There have been numerous accounts of this. In an ill-fated expedition in the arctic, men huddled together nearly naked. It's one of the rules of survival, learned of experience and based on sound physical principles. If you want to freeze two steaks quickly in the freezer, you separate them."

"Thank you, Colonel."

The Deputy Prosecutor, Mr. Perkins, began his questioning.
"Col. Ross, are you acquainted with the defendant?"
"Yes".
"Could you explain the basis, the extent of this acquaintance?"
"Certainly. A couple of months ago, Mr. Plotkin contacted me to ask about my willingness to research and testify about this event. I had been referred by a mutual friend in the Army, with whom Mr. Plotkin had served in the Adjutant General's office. I first met Mr. Cross a few weeks ago, when I interviewed him at length on two occasions, about the events on Mt. Baker. That is the extent of our acquaintance."

"Would you say that, as a result of this acquaintance, you are favorably disposed toward Mr. Cross?"

"I find him to be a likeable, an admirable, person. But I retain my capacity to be objective in my testimony."

"Col. Ross, you have spoken of the events on the mountain. You expressed your opinion on the difficulty in skiing down the mountain from the site where the girl was found. Have you personally surveyed the site?"

"My skiing days are over. It's called ortheoarthritis. But the commanding officer at Fort Lewis kindly put at our disposal two expert skiers, volunteers from the 1ˢᵗ Special Forces Group, Airborne. They surveyed the area in question, matching his GPS coordinates ..."

"His?"

"Mr. Cross's. All this is in your discovery, Mr. Perkins, and is in Sergeant Nolan's deposition, which the court has heard. We matched Mr. Cross's readings against our maps, from the parking area, to the hut, to the place where Miss Noll was found, back to the hut, then to the base again. I'm satisfied that his account is accurate. I could find no inconsistency in his and Miss Noll's accounts"...now he turned to face the jury ..."and neither could the Army's Special Forces."

"Colonel, why was it necessary for them to go to the hut at all?"

"He had four alternatives. Understand that he was faced with saving the life of a young girl, who had somehow, against the odds, survived the first night alone, and appeared to be suffering from hypothermia. He had to get her warm, and off the mountain, and into a hospital. If he had skied away to let the search parties find her, or to try to connect with the search parties, she would have died the second night. No question. He did not consider that as an alternative at all.

First, they could have stayed where Miss Noll spent the first night, in their snow cave, and waited for rescuers. But no one was looking there. They had the red flasher, nothing else to signal or communicate. They had only the food and fuel that he had carried. They might have survived for two or three days. They had no shelter, only a small snow cave that he built with his hands, and a five-by-seven foot thermal blanket that was intended for one person. The searchers, in fact, never reached this point. This clearly was not a good alternative.

Second, heading to the west, where Miss Noll had come from, might have put them in contact with searchers, had they extended their search to the east of the area where the concentration of searchers were. But she had covered this ground, most of it on skis, moving fast. Mr. Cross and Miss Noll would be hampered by walking, or attempting to move on one pair of skis, with the difficulty that this presented. And if they failed to meet up with searchers, they would have died. The search, in fact, did not extend far enough that they conceivably would have met. So he was wise in not choosing this alternative, also.

Third, they could have tried to go straight down from there, to meet up with the Mt. Baker Highway – in a straight line, it is closer objective than the other alternatives presented. But the terrain is such that even experienced skiers would not attempt it; it is all precipices. His topo map told him that.

Fourth, going to the hut, was the only good alternative. He knew where it was. And they had food, shelter and fuel there, even if limited. He knew the route to the hut, and from there to the road. He had only the difficulty of getting them both there, then down to the road, to contend with.

The court has heard a deposition made by an experienced Nordic skier, one of the two Special Forces volunteers. They retraced on skis the route that Mr. Cross and Miss Noll followed. I believe that the significant statement is – here he read from notes in his hand. This is from Sergeant Nolan Nelson, the senior of the two. 'Sir, I'm a good skier, and I wouldn't want to try carrying another person down that mountain, after that snowstorm, even a child. I could do it, but I don't see how he did it in the time he did, with the weather and snow conditions that he faced. The angels must have been with them.'"

The courtroom was still. The prosecutors were frozen. They knew it was all over. Can we just get out of here?

"Let's move on to the activities in the cabin. Colonel, you drew the analogy of the Arctic expedition. Was there a woman in the expedition?" Groans came from the spectators.

Ray stayed in his seat, amused. Let him dig himself into a hole, he thought.

"There was not."

"Had there been one, do you think that she would have huddled, naked, with the men?"

"If she wanted to survive, she would have. Hypothermia and the fact of facing death do not excite the libido. And that is what our two were facing."

"So you think that 'our two' should have been naked?" There was an uproar from the spectators. The word "asshole" came through clearly.

Judge: "There will be order in the court!"

Ross looked at the Deputy Prosecutor as if he were a worm. "Of course not -- out of moral considerations, as well as lack of necessity. Clothed as they were, they were able to retain sufficient heat. In effect, each was wearing a nightshirt and underclothing, with only their legs bare. Conditions were below freezing, but not 50 degrees below. We are talking about a young girl here. I believe that Mr. Cross acted with propriety, as well as with prudence."

"But why not pants?"

"Wearing pants would have defeated the purpose of retaining warmth, flesh on flesh. Also, their pants, like their jackets, were encrusted with ice. Would you have them put on icy ski pants, in their bed? I don't think so."

"But why couldn't they have dried them out on the stove?"

Ross took a deep breath, then looked at Perkins for a few seconds with disdain. "The hut was barely above freezing during the day, and well below at night. The heating and cooking stove had been installed, but the owner had not made it operational because of a faulty flue, and so he had concerns over carbon monoxide poisoning. Mr. Cross had been told that, and that's why there was no fuel supply. Their leftover evening milk tea was frozen, on the floor by their bed, the next morning.

"But Mr. Cross's account says that they melted snow, cooked dehydrated foods, canned soups, tea…and heated their famous bathwater… How did they do this, without a stove?"

Ross looked at the Deputy Prosecutor as though he were explaining something to a small child. He spoke slowly and deliberately. "Cooking in the hut was done with the same stove that he had used in the snow cave, carried in his backpack. It is called a Primus, Mr. Perkins. It is about the size of a small melon, and functions to heat pans of water and food. It cannot function as a space heater or a clothes dryer."

The red-faced and shaken Deputy Prosecutor said, "Thank you, that's all, Mr…ah ..Colonel Ross."

Judge: "Thank you, Colonel. You may step down."

Every eye was on Andrew, as the tall, dignified old soldier stood and strode to his seat.

*   *   *

The next afternoon, the jury announced its verdict.

I was pronounced not guilty of both charges, kidnapping and molestation. The judge ordered that both convictions be vacated. Missy was crying, and we were hugging each other and Ray and Nancy so hard that I heard only part of what the judge said. But it was something about, in his two decades on the bench, he had never seen such an appalling miscarriage of justice…

When he slammed down the gavel in loud, final decision as the court was dismissed, a tanker in Bellingham Bay laid down a long, low, flat blast as if to signal the end of this ordeal, this unspeakable exercise in iniquity.

Cries, laughter, hugs and tears circled the defense table as spectators and friends gathered and joined in widening circles, as if in a dancing feast of celebration.

And the pack of prosecutors, their necks sloped like hyenas chased from the feast by lions, slunk off in silence, back to their darkness, beyond the touching light of the angels.

Missy and I were vindicated.

Nogales was in jail and Graber was dead.

The judge stepped down and walked over to us. He spoke quietly with Missy for a moment.

I heard, "You're a wonderful and courageous person. We expect more good things from you…Good luck in your studies…and you let me know if I can ever be of help.." Then he turned, and smiled as he grabbed my hand in a tight grip. He acknowledged Ray and Nancy, and, "Thank you, Colonel."

The bailiff told me later, "He never does that!"

That day we knew that Truth and Beauty were in the world, even if sometimes, accompanied by Justice, they went out for a very long break.

That night, Ray invited all of us to dinner. All I really remember is that when we were getting ready to leave, and I was talking to Andrew about picking him up in the morning to take him to the airport, Missy came over and interrupted. Andrew stood, and Missy thanked him, then she wrapped her arms around his waist and hugged him tightly, as his big arms went around her shoulders. Missy had not forgotten the numbing cold, the terror, the near-death. Andrew was the only person other than I who really understood what had happened on the mountain

"I'm sorry," Missy said, as she saw that her tears had wet his shirt.

"I will never wash this shirt again," replied Lieutenant Colonel Ross.

Ray contacted the editor of the ski magazine, and asked for a retraction. The magazine put a reporter on it; she asked for more information. And a few months later, we saw that we got not the usual one column-inch, grudging apology, but a full article, leading off with their first reportage, and subsequent events. We had provided some photos. It made a wonderful story.

CHAPTER FIFTEEN ─────────────

MISSY AND I PLANNED A few quiet days together. She had a school vacation, and I arranged with Felix for him and Abe to cover for me. He agreed that I needed some time off after the trial.

The cabin was nearly finished. All the structural stuff was done; it was just a matter of doing small things. The workmen were coming and going on an irregular basis. I was doing all the electrical work myself, but I couldn't do plumbing and other things.

The cabin had a central room, a combination dining and living room; at the end was a real stone fireplace. A local guy, a retired mason, had built it in his own good time. "I don't do this any more, but as long as you're not in a hurry..." I was finding some good neighbors here. There was an antique glass globe with a wrought iron chandelier hanging in the middle of the room. An old sofa and chairs were already in place in front of the fireplace. There was a corner in the main room with bookshelves and a writing table.

The dining table was a small one with extension leaves, and four chairs, all bought at a thrift shop. It was placed under the old chandelier.

The cabin had a small kitchen; the stove wasn't in yet, so I used a camping stove with a butane cartridge, and a large cast-iron Dutch oven for baking, and for making stews. There was a tiny refrigerator that I had borrowed from the office, as no one used it. The kitchen was basic, but all we needed for our cooking.

There was one bedroom plus a sleeping loft with two beds; this was for the boys when they came to visit. The plumbing was in, and the water running.

There was a flash water heater, and a shower in the one small bathroom. So we had our basic comforts, and planned to spend much of our time doing mostly detail work, sanding and painting. This would be a great cabin when we were finished.

I remember now that our staying together in the cabin then, with Missy working alongside me investing in the cabin also, told both of us that we would share this with everything else in our lives. It wasn't my cabin, it was ours; this was unspoken.

I had picked her up at her boarding house about noon; on the way to the Nooksack, we stopped at a market for groceries. I planned my special veal stew for our first supper in the cabin together, and I bought a good bottle of burgundy.

As we entered the cabin and unloaded our things and Missy looked around, I carried her bag up to the sleeping loft. We busied ourselves for a while, mostly my taking her on a tour, showing her what worked and didn't yet, what this is for, and that, and my plans for this corner and the other one. Then we took a walk outside, around the cabin; I showed her where the generator was and how to start it, and then we stood for a while looking at the river.

I seated her on the small porch overlooking the river. "We'll have a glass of wine with dinner, if you like. But now, some tea? Soft drink?"

"Just water is ok," she said.

"I'm going to start the stew, because it takes a while. Once it starts, we can take a walk."

"May I help you cook?"

Missy wanted to chop the vegetables. I heated the Dutch oven on the burner, added a little peanut oil, and began browning the small pieces of veal. When they were finished, I poured out the oil, then added some dry white wine, and Missy's carrots, onions and garlic cloves. Then a can of Italian tomatoes, a couple of bay leaves, dried thyme, salt and freshly ground pepper. I boiled all this for a moment, then put the lid on the big pot, and turned the flame very low. I opened the bottle of burgundy.

"Ok. This will be ok for a while." Then we went for a walk. There was a trail on the edge of the rushing river, passing through old-growth forest, with lots of moss and climbing ivy and fallen trees. I lifted her onto the trunk of a tree that crossed our path; it put our faces even, and I told her about everything in the woods and on the river that I could remember. I told her of my surprise meeting with two black bears early one morning on the trail: a sow and a yearling cub almost her size, were running up the trail like children at play. Then they spotted or sniffed me, and mom turned the cub around with her snout, grunting, and they quickly trotted away.

Missy and I continued walking beside the river until the light started to fade, and we were tripping over roots and rocks in the path. Then we turned back and returned to the cabin.

I set the Dutch oven aside, and put an aluminum pan on the burner, half full of water. I added salt and a bit of olive oil, and turned the flame up, to boil our fettuccini. Missy set the table, putting out two wine glasses. I chopped a bit of parsley.

I warmed a couple of plates with hot water, and put them on the table. Then I served the drained fettuccini, then the veal with its sauce on top, and sprinkled it with the parsley. I poured the wine, and we sat down.

"Oh!" Missy cried, jumping up. "We should have these!" She had spotted a couple of candles in holders on the fireplace mantle, and brought them over. I lit the candles, then turned down the dimmer on the chandelier. Missy glowed with happiness.

We ate the stew in silence. When our eyes met for a moment, we glanced away.

"I didn't make any dessert!" I said. "But we've got some strawberry ice cream in the fridge!"

Missy didn't say anything at first, but kept eating quietly, a flush in her cheeks. "That will be great," she said.

After a while, the spell was over. "Oh, Hamlin, that was delicious! Make it again for me! But let's take a walk down to the river, before we have ice cream, ok?"

We walked down to the bank of the Nooksack in front of our cabin and saw and heard the gushing of the glacial runoff hurtling over rocks, and smashing against whole trees fallen across part of the river. I was thinking about our kinship with the river. It flows from where we met. She said at the same time, "Do you think that that is our ice and snow that is melted there? Could it sit up there for six years before it decided to come down to meet us? I think that it is saying, 'It's really good to see you again, but we can't stop! We're going to the ocean now!'" I took her hand and we walked back to the cabin for our strawberry ice cream.

Missy insisted on tidying up the dishes. I got some paper and kindling, and a couple of small logs, and started a fire. Then we took turns in the shower, and got into pajamas and robes. I fixed coffee, and set out a decanter of good port, and brought down some books.

We sat on the old couch, and looked over the choice of books. She wanted

Robert Frost, first. "The poem about the little horse who shakes his bells!" I knew that she knew the poem as well as I did, and was teasing. While I was looking for the poem, she spied the port. "What's that?"

"It's port wine. It's grape wine that has brandy added. So it's stronger than usual wine; that's why we use such small glasses. You only sip." And I poured her a bit, and she tasted just a little.

I read the poem. She looked at me as she had when I first read it to her, years before. We really must go to New Hampshire, and take that snowy ride in a sleigh pulled by a small horse! Then I read "The Call of the Yukon", and she snuggled against me, and I put my arm around her. After a while, I stopped reading, and we looked at the fire for a while. And we napped. Then I got up and poked out the fire. She watched me quietly as the room began to darken. And we both knew that she was not going to the sleeping loft. I took her hand, and we went to bed.

We went back to the hours of years ago, as though there had been no interval, when we had wrapped ourselves together for warmth. And I knew that all the suffering, the deprivation, the pain of the prison years, was nothing compared to the joy of having Missy close to me again. But it was different this time.

*　　　　*　　　　*

Years later, I remembered that this evening was really the beginning. As beautiful as were the first days of our meeting, the era of the snow cave and Lee's hut was over. The red curls now framed the face of a beautiful young woman, no longer a pretty little girl. The snuggling and warm affection were a pleasant memory, and added to by something much stronger. Before the night was over, we knew that we were in love with each other, and that we always would be, and we told each other so. And these declarations set the course of the rest of our lives.

It was a week of joy. We went back to Bellingham a couple of times, and had lunch and dinner in Fairhaven, the historic district, and went to the U to walk around, and to visit friends. We worked on the cabin, and when we rested, we lay on the big bed and hugged and napped. We pulled down books, and read to each other. She had to read aloud Robert Service's "The Shooting of Dan McGrew" with all of the flair and drama. We finished *The Wind in the Willows*; we both remembered where we had stopped, in Lee's hut. We hiked up and down the trails by the side of the river and ate small sandwiches and munched on apple halves as we looked at the incredible beauty of what God had put on both sides of the Nooksack, and the huge glacier above.

Once we drove by the ranger station which Missy didn't remember, and then up as far as we could drive on the mountain to the Heather Meadows, to walk among the tiny lakes, the spotty summer snow fields, and the gentle and fragile blue flowers by the side of the path.

We had long talks.

When Missy spoke of Claire and Arthur and their families, she always used the present tense; all others who had been in her life were history. So there were two unburned bridges. I was glad that she had them. They were really her only family; she never spoke of the people in her own house.

"Claire's dad is a big shot in the Navy, a Rear Admiral. Her mom is Korean. They are really nice and refined people. They treated me so well!

Well, when we kids would come over to Claire's house on Saturdays, if her dad were at home, he would make a dish that he called 'slumgummy.' He said that it's a traditional Irish supper. I researched it in the library and found 'slumgullion,' which is a 'meat stew.' I won't tell you what the dictionary said about the word derivation. Anyway, it was ground beef, onions, tomatoes and kidney beans, with some garlic and spices, all done in a big frying pan. I know because I watched him make it one night. It was always delicious! That and his garlic bread. It was so heavy with garlic and butter that it was hard to pick up! He wanted us to eat lots – he said that 'If you go away hungry, the house gets a bad name!'

If he weren't there, her mom would make different things, but I remember her chicken stew; she would drop spoons of batter on top of it and cover the pot until they were baked into dumplings. And her rhubarb and raisin pudding!

Everyone says that Claire got the best of both worlds – she is truly beautiful, not just pretty.

And she plays the piano, very well. Also, she was the head of the drama club at our high school, and had the role of Beauty in the annual play, *The Beauty and the Beast*. But because she is so talented, the school paper wrote that she could have played the Beast as well! Anyway, she's my best friend, except maybe for Arthur. But we're all three best friends, equally!" She showed me the picture.

The picture was of a handsome, if skinny, boy facing the camera, with the two girls in profile, each kissing one of Arthur's cheeks, as Missy made rabbit ears behind his head. Three beautiful, clean kids. I loved the picture, and today it has its pride of place on our mantle, enclosed in a rectangular silver frame.

"Arthur's parents came from Russia. His dad is an electronics engineer, and his mom a piano teacher. She played with the Moscow Symphony Orchestra or something. And she's a great cook! There was always something delicious on the table whenever we went over there after school, or on weekends. And his dad and mom played music together after dinner -- he had a stringed instrument, something like a balalaika, but I don't remember what it was called. Often Claire would sit in at the piano; she was their protégé, learning and playing traditional Russian melodies. Arthur's mom would look on, smiling so proudly and beautifully as Claire accompanied him on one tune after another."

Missy was in a happy reverie, thinking of dinner at Arthur's and Claire's homes. She didn't speak of dinner at her own house.

Chapter Sixteen ─────────────

Missy told me that her parents were in town; she had received numerous phone messages at her boarding house while we were at the cabin. She called the hotel number that was left, and talked to her mom. They wanted to see her, Mom explained. Missy agreed, but said that I would be with her. Mom didn't like the idea. Missy said that that's the condition.

I said, "Missy, I don't see any need for me to meet with them. They are your parents, and I'm sure they don't have any love for me."

"Hamlin, he is big and he is mean. He played football at USC and doesn't let anyone forget it. And he's very angry over the whole thing."

"So why do you want to meet with them?"

She thought for a moment. "For closure. After this, we have nothing else to talk about, ever."

"Ok. I'll go with you."

"Hamlin, I told her that if he puts a hand on you or me, he will go to jail, now. We are known here, and they are not. This isn't San Diego."

They were staying in the most expensive hotel in Bellingham, in the penthouse, top floor but for the revolving restaurant above. Mom, an agitated, ferret-faced woman, answered the door. After she introduced herself, she presented Russ, Missy's brother, who was on his way out the door. He was a thick, loutish-looking twenty-something, with a prominent scar across his right cheek and nose. A grumbled "How's it going, man?" was his idea of an introductory greeting. He and Missy exchanged neither a glance nor a word as he pushed his way out the door behind us.

We were led to the living room, where Dad sat with a drink in his hand, in one of eight overstuffed white chairs around a square black marble coffee table. It looked like the setting for a meeting of crime bosses.

Dad put down his drink slowly, and got up with a delay calculated to say that meeting with us was an unwelcome interruption to his important routine. His look exuded a lack of sobriety and intelligence.

He sized me up physically, with a practiced look. I'm not small, but he had almost two inches in height, and about forty pounds on me; much of it looked like fat. He tried to impress me with his hand crush as we shook. I wondered briefly how my beautiful, graceful and intelligent girl could have been fathered by this big fool.

We seated ourselves with Missy between Mom and me. I was careful, after what Missy had said, to place myself as a buffer between her and Dad. Mom gestured where we were to sit, but I ignored her instructions, as I guided Missy by her elbow to the seating of my choice. Dad gave me a quick look of anger as he saw that they had been outsmarted. Not a good start for a congenial meeting, I thought.

"So, what do you do, Mr. Cross?" Mom asked coldly but politely.

"I'm an electrician," I replied.

Dad snorted, with a smirk.

"So you two are friends, now?" Mom asked.

"He is my good friend," Missy replied. Another snort from Dad. I turned to him, and he looked away and picked up his drink.

As if to explain, Missy said, "I'm staying in a women's boarding house near the U."

"Yes, we know your address!" said Mom. "We also know that you haven't been there for the past week!"

Missy said nothing.

"So, where were you?"

"Are you asking me because you have suddenly become interested in my life, or because you think that I still have to report in to you?"

"Don't you talk to your mother that way!" snarled Dad.

Missy regarded him with cool contempt. "Do you know that I am eighteen, and emancipated? You requested this meeting. Neither of us feels the need for it. I don't owe either of you an explanation for anything." Missy was beautiful. She had these two under her complete control.

"Don't you..." Dad started again, but stopped, confused. He didn't know how to finish his sentence.

Missy continued. "If you really want to know, it was a school vacation, so I went with Hamlin to the cabin that he's building on the Nooksack River."

"So it's 'Hamlin,' now!" laughed Dad.

"That's my name," I said, looking at him straight.

"I guess we know what you did there for a week," sneered Mom.

"No, you don't know. You don't know anything. So I'll tell you."

"You watch your mouth, young lady!" growled Dad.

"We spent the days working on the cabin, and when we rested, we read to each other. And we cooked. He gave me lessons -- he's really a great cook! And we went into Bellingham, and Fairhaven, and went to bookstores, and just fooled around, and threw a Frisbee in the park, and visited friends. And at night, we did what you and the CPS and the police and the court and the newspapers said we did six years ago, but this time we really did it. Three times a night -- actually, sometimes four."

Dad looked as though he wanted to kill. Mom was speechless, for a moment, and then:

"You were captain of the school debating team! You won the state championship!"

"And neither of you were there! Did you happen to read about it in the newspaper?"

Mom ignored this and continued:

"You were a National Merit Scholar! You would have been the class valedictorian! You were accepted by three top universities. And you're giving all that up for...him? An electrician?" She tossed a contemptuous look and gesture at me.

"I *am* a National Merit Scholar. And I *have been* accepted by three top universities. And, he's not an electrician, he's a graduate electrical engineer. With a masters degree also. That's something you won't find on the wall in your house. What I'm doing is called 'flight to quality,' Mom. You can have the broker translate that for you. And I'm still going to college."

The broker? Again.

Dad was stunned into silence. He had to do something, but didn't know what.

Mom spit, "You'll get nothing from us for college!" as if fixing Missy's fate forever.

Missy laughed easily, catching my eye with her glint that said, do you see the humor in this that I see?

"We don't need your money."

119

The "we" gave my heart a happy little extra beat.

But Mom had a different take on "we."

"*We?*" So you're screwing for money! I guess that makes you a common whore!"

"Time to go, Missy." I said, standing up.

"You go," said Dad. "We're still talking."

Missy was hammering her knees with her fists, and starting to get teary. "Mom, you tried to use me, your own daughter, to ruin a good and decent man, who saved my life! You were part of that big lie that put him in prison! But you can't destroy Hamlin Cross, because he's a *man*! And," she said, glaring at Dad, "he's *not*!"

This was too much. Dad stood up unsteadily and started to advance toward Missy. I pushed back my chair and stepped in front of him. "Get out of my way," he said quietly. I looked straight in his eyes.

Abe had said, "Conversation has no place in a fight. It's a distraction. Keep your mouth shut." So I continued to stare into his eyes, while being mindful of our distance, and my stance.

"You think you're pretty tough, pervert?" I continued to look into his eyes. You talk, I thought. Abe, don't fail me now.

He sent me an e-mail about the punch. The subject was "roundhouse right." I easily slipped it, stepped in, and hit him solidly just below his left ear. He stumbled, dazed, for a few seconds, then recovered. Now there was real fear in his eyes. But there was no turning back. He stepped back a foot, then charged in a rage, his big arms flailing. It was my turn to be afraid, as I saw the weight and power of big muscle and bones looking for me. But I dropped low and sidestepped him, and guided him onto the coffee table. He went over and down with a crash, taking out the entire coffee service, his huge limbs inelegantly splayed over the table. He lay as he fell for a moment, an ugly relief on the marble square.

"Holy shit!" breathed Missy.

After a few seconds, he recovered and picked himself up, slipping on the coffee-slick table. His front was soaked with coffee and festooned with porcelain chips and sugar cubes. Then he came looking for me, as would a confused and fatigued bull in its last moments, thinking, where is that pesky matador, anyway? I had positioned myself away from the table and chairs, and when he rushed me again, I simply tripped him as I stepped aside, and he went down on all fours. As he started to get up, I punched him very hard again just under his left ear, and he went back down on his knees, where he reposed as if in prayer. That was where I wanted him to be, so that we could talk.

My right hand grabbed the back of his blazer collar, and my forearm whipped across his throat. My left hand grabbed his lapel, loosely, at the ready. I watched his eyes, and waited for them to focus. Then I spoke quietly into his left ear.

"Listen carefully. If you ever make a move on me again, or God help you, against my Missy, I will break every bone in your body. Have I made my position clear?"

He nodded dumbly.

Mom was a mannequin.

"Let's go, Missy," I said, dropping his head and stepping away.

The Meeting With The Parents was over.

In the elevator, Missy stood with her back against the wall, her hands splayed flat on the mirrored surface. She looked at me as though I were a god, just descended from Mount Olympus.

"Holy shit!"

"Watch your language, squirt," I said, giving her a rough kiss.

"Hamlin, I've never seen anyone make him back down, not even in an argument, much less beat him up!"

"That wasn't a beating, Missy, it was only an admonition. I wouldn't beat up anyone in front of his child."

She gave me a quick, strange glance, then looked away. "But what did you say to him? I couldn't hear."

"Oh, just guy talk."

"No, really, I want to know!"

"I told him that if he ever touched you again, he would be the 'Soup of the Day'".

She gave me an amused and grateful smile. But the "again" passed without comment; she had unwittingly confirmed my pretty good guess.

CHAPTER SEVENTEEN ─────────

I PICKED MISSY UP FOR lunch. I had asked her to bring a change of clothes, as we would be exercising in the park, and later go out to dinner.

We went to a Vietnamese restaurant. Missy said, "I've never had Vietnamese food before."

"Then let me order, ok?" Phô was a bowl of broth with noodles, and thinly-sliced beef, covered with fresh sprouts, basil, mint and a chunk of lime. There was some spicy red sauce on the side. The restaurant served that and nothing else. Nothing else was needed nor wanted.

As she worked her chopsticks to dredge up the noodles, she asked, "How could we have gone to war with people who make such delicious food?"

I thought for a moment. "German, Japanese, Mexican, Italian, Chinese, Korean ...the people that we have fought with have given us our favorite foods. The English may be an exception."

"You're goofy!" she laughed. "Hey, don't forget fish and chips! And we must have gotten meat loaf from somewhere... Well, anyway, if it hadn't been for the war, there wouldn't be so many Vietnamese over here, and we wouldn't have this great food. So maybe the war was over the soup?"

"We'll call this 'Missy's Food Fight Theory of History.' But I'd rather have the food without the fight. Like Indian. We didn't have to go to war with India to get curry. And mulligatawny – that's the soup!"

"You haven't made it for me!"

When we finished and paid, we walked back to the van that said "Whatcom Home Security." It had red and blue ladders on top, and orange cones stacked on the front bumper. It looked like a psychedelic rhinoceros. "Someday, my princess, I will transport you in something much more elegant."

"Like a crystal carriage? Pulled by a team of white ponies with pompoms on their heads?"

"That's almost a promise!"

We went to Boulevard Park, a noodle-shaped park between Bellingham Bay and the city. I had brought a Frisbee and softball. And a book of poetry, and a thermos of hot chocolate and cups, all in a backpack.

We spent much of the afternoon playing catch with the softball, having ditched the Frisbee after the first half-hour. There were too many flying, like planes in an airport with no controller, and dogs were snatching ours. "No, Hunter! That's not ours! Put it down! Good dog!"

When we tired of catch, we sat at one of the large picnic tables, straddling the same bench. And we took turns reading from the *One Hundred and One Famous Poems*. Then she asked me to recite "Kublai Khan," which, like "Jabberwocky" and "The Owl and the Pussycat," I had committed to memory. Wow. When I finished, I poured some hot chocolate. We sipped and watched the children and dogs playing.

"Hamlin, you recite these poems with such…feeling! Almost as though you were there! And saw everything!"

"Missy, that's what the authors want us to feel!" I didn't tell her that I had worked on my elocution in Monroe State Reformatory.

As the light faded, we joined the others leaving the park and we went back to the van, and to my apartment.

While Missy showered, I busied myself on a project on my PC. When she came out, she saw me hunched over the keyboard and eyeing the screen, and asked if she could have something to drink. "Sorry, I've forgotten my manners. I'll get you a Coke or what?"

"No, I would like a glass of wine while I am waiting," she said, a bit petulantly. With some trepidation, I poured her a glass of Chablis.

She had put on clean jeans and an auburn silk shirt with a black vest. Her hair was pulled back with a headband. A neat black jacket was lying on the sofa arm. I was looking forward to showing her off this evening. She was understated classy, as only a very young woman can be. And I suddenly thought that she had no jewelry, almost no accessories. She really had just graduated from a backpack. I would do something about that, soon.

I was taking care of all her expenses, and we had repaid the loans from her school friends. She knew that she had not compromised herself by accepting my support; our bond was strong enough that that would never be an issue.

The glass of wine was in her hand, and she was leaning back on the sofa in a relaxed, mature pose. "What are you writing?"

"It's a love story."

"What is his name?"

"Hamlin."

"What's hers?"

"Haven't decided yet."

Missy put down her glass and got up and went over to me.

"Hey, I'm writing! Don't you know writers are temperamental?"

"They are also smelly!" she said, sniffing my neck. "Are you taking me to dinner or what?" I stood up, then picked her up and flipped her horizontally, spun around a couple of times, then dropped her gently on the sofa. Her face was flushed, and had the love look on again. I kissed her gently on her lips.

"I'm going to shower."

"May I watch?"

*   *   *

We had reservations at Chez Robert, the restaurant where students take their visiting parents. We were taken to a secluded corner that I had requested. As we passed through the room, there were smiles and whispers of recognition, and a "Hi, Missy!" from a school friend. A big thumbs-up from someone else. Missy said quietly, "Are we celebrities? Should we give autographs?" She was enjoying the fame.

We were seated near an older couple, who beamed their approval of our presence: uncle and niece, or elder brother and sister, she a WWU student, he visiting, having a dinner out. I ordered fruit juice for Missy, and a glass of Chablis for myself, while we looked at the menus.

Every now and then, Missy would switch our glasses for a sip. The neighbors smiled at the subterfuge.

Missy and I were holding our thoughts. I think now that we both knew how this evening would end, but weren't sure about the protocol. So we fumbled for a while.

"Why did you tell your parents that we did it?"

"I think the word is 'closure.'" Again. "Don't ask me why! To shut them off forever. Do you remember what Robert Redford, or was it Paul Newman, said in '*The Sting*'?—that it's more satisfying if they don't know that they have been stung, or something like that!"

"As you further develop your beautiful character, you will learn that compassion and forgiveness are worthy qualities." She looked at me, annoyed at my pedantic and preachy tone, and at the fact that I had pointed the conversation in a useless direction.

"But I don't want to further develop my character, or do anything else, without *you!*" And she hit the table with her fist on "you!" and the dishes bounced. The couple at the next table glanced. Maybe they are not family?

I knew that we were heading into new territory.

She leaned closely over the table. "Why didn't we do it, really, at the Nooksack?" I was glad that the neighbors could hear only the ballistics, and not the conversation.

"Because we would have betrayed the angels." She frowned in concentration; it reminded me of Franklin, when his little brow had furrowed as he pondered a difficult problem with a toy. "Because we wanted to preserve the innocence of our first stay together, in the snow cave and Lee's hut."

She examined a piece of bread for a few seconds.

"Where do you think the angels were?"

"Well, one was on the slopes guiding me to you, and one was in San Diego, and one was in Bellingham. And one was in Kirkland long ago." I didn't tell her about the angel's visit to Monroe.

"Do you think it's like duty stations? Do they get rotations?"

"In Japan, there is a thousand year-old shrine, Izumo, in the city of Matsue. Every year, the gods from all over Japan visit, like having a convention. I've been there. And going down a walkway to the shrine, you can see what look like martin houses, where the gods, or spirits, stay during their visit. And a god from Hokkaido will say that there is a farmer whose son is looking for a wife, and another will say that there is a fisherman from Shikoku who has a young daughter, and a god from Kyoto will have... And during the meeting they make arrangements, sometimes business stuff, sometimes personal things, and sort things out, and help people, I guess as our angels helped us."

"Do you mean that our American angels have adopted the Japanese management system?" This was said loudly, much to the amusement of the neighbors. I took my wine glass back.

Our entrees came, and we picked at our choices. "Hamlin," she whispered, "You make much better veal stew than this!"

"Thanks, Missy," I said, as I took a fork and steak knife to my poached salmon. What time does this plane land?, I wondered.

When the meal was out of the way, we skipped the supermarket tiramisu in favor of just coffee. We looked at each other. So?

"This is the thing," she said, having retired the fist for a forefinger stabbing the table. "The Japanese spirits were really matchmakers, right? So maybe, just maybe, our angels are waiting for us to do something?"

There was a long interval. Then she knocked over my nearly-empty wine glass as her hands moved toward mine, and we grasped tightly. Our eyes held. Then she said evenly, "What do you think would make the angels happy?"

"If we did it with rings on."

> "But what shall we do for a ring?
> They sailed away for a year and a day,
> To the land where the bong tree grows;
> And there in a wood, a piggy-wig stood,
> With a ring in the end of his nose.
> 'Dear pig, are you willing to sell for one shilling,
> Your ring?' Said the piggy, 'I will.'
> So they took it away, and were married next day
> By the turkey that lives on the hill…'"

I asked "Are there bong trees in Bellingham?"

"No, but I know a place that has conventional rings, not piggy-wig aftermarket," she laughed through her beginning tears.

As we left the restaurant, this time to light applause, Missy wrapped both arms around one of mine. We walked toward the van. "Are you ok for lunch tomorrow, and the afternoon free?" She nodded. "We have some big shopping to do, and an important event to schedule."

She pulled me to a stop, and then stepped in front, placing her hands flat on my chest. Then her hands were balled into fists at her side. "Hamlin! *Hamlin!*" she shouted, almost fiercely, then reached up to grab me around my neck with both arms, pulling me down to her.

And an angel in the wheelhouse of a freighter in Bellingham Bay triggered a long four-blast salute as Missy buried her wet face in my shoulder and we hugged tightly. And we stood that way for a long, long time.

CHAPTER EIGHTEEN ───────────

I MET MISSY AFTER HER morning classes, and we had a soup and salad lunch in the school cafeteria. She wouldn't eat, just picked at her salad. There was something big on her mind.

"Before we go shopping, can we go to the park for a little while?"

I was worried. Angels, please don't let me lose her now. We were on our way to buy a ring!

At Boulevard Park, we sat at a big picnic table. She asked me to sit on one bench, then ran around and sat down on the other side. It was too far across the table. I felt as though we were North and South Korean delegates getting positioned for one of their pissing matches. Missing were only the flags, guards and guns. She had seated us like this for a reason.

"Hamlin, there is something I have to tell you." She waited. "No, two things.

First, he's not my father. My dad died when I was six, and Mom remarried about a year after, I guess. I never liked Fred, and the feeling was mutual. He came with a son, Russ – just like him, and two years older than I."

Missy stopped for a while, and looked at the table.

"Mom changed - she became more like Fred. The idea that I heard from counselors was that I rejected him because he couldn't replace my father. This is bs. As much as I had loved my dad, I could have accepted, after a while, anyway, a stepfather. I just couldn't accept *him*! I refuse to this day to call him 'Dad.' They wouldn't let me call him 'Fred.' So I didn't call him anything!"

"For eleven years?"

"Yes! If I had to refer to him, he was 'the broker.' Because he's a stockbroker. He was chronically pissed off at me!"

I wonder why, I thought.

"Did he beat you?"

"No, but he shook me a lot when I was little, and when I got older, he slapped me. And for no reason, or for really trivial stuff. I can't say that he beat me, like nothing that left marks."

"Did he molest you?"

A Frisbee landed on our table, and slid off the end, chased by a couple of laughing children. "Sorry!" they sang. We were distracted for a moment.

"Who?"

"Fred!"

"No."

"I think that you may have just saved his life, Missy. But didn't your mother protect you?"

"She couldn't even protect herself! He was much rougher on her, than on me! The only person he didn't hit was my stepbrother, because he was a jock, and they were sports buddies. And he was his son, after all!"

"What do you remember about your dad?"

She paused. "That he was the greatest and strongest and gentlest person in my life. He was a marine biologist. He would take me early in the morning and late in the afternoon, to walk on the beach, in our bare feet. He would pick up each tiny creature and let me hold it in my hand, and tell me how it lived. He held me on his lap and read stories and poetry to me. He taught me things. No," she said, waving the thought away. "Don't think father-substitute stuff. I've been through all that. But," she smiled, "I know that you would have been the best of friends!" She sat looking at the table, silently, the smile lingering.

"And the other thing?"

She waited. Now she was drawing circles in the condensation on the lacquered top of the knotted pine table.

She looked at me as would a child who expects to be punished. She bit her lip.

"See, I didn't get lost. I ran away. To get away from those people, and maybe to meet my Dad in heaven. When Dad died, my aunt told me that he's with the angels in heaven. I asked too many questions, and she gave me kind of an awkward explanation that he's walking on the clouds with the angels. A while later, when my Mom and I were flying somewhere, I had a window seat, like most kids want, but I wanted to look for my Dad on the clouds. And the stew said to close the shades because they were going to show a movie, or something. I wouldn't do it. My Mom can be bitchy with other people too, so there was a big fight and I think she nearly got arrested, stopping the stew from closing my window shade.

Well, we had come from San Diego, for a sales convention or something that Fred had in Bellingham, and we were on a ski package, on Mt. Baker. The mountain was all clouds and snow, and I was feeling especially down. I'd been punished for something, I don't remember what. My stepbrother, Russ, was the champion skier, and everyone was making a fuss over him. I had the 'nobody loves me' feeling that every kid gets sometime, and my braces had been adjusted a couple days before, and my teeth hurt. And I was on my XC skis, and a thought just entered my mind, like an angel landed on my shoulder talking to me, to get out of there, away from those people forever. So I just skied away, and nobody noticed. I didn't know what would happen, but when I saw the clouds I was heading into, I thought I would die or meet my Dad. So I just kept on going. I didn't stop, I kept on going all day. I didn't go up, and I didn't go down. I hadn't brought anything with me, except a water bottle and an energy bar.

Then one of the bindings on my skis broke. I didn't know how to fix it, and I had no tools anyway, so I had to leave it. I couldn't do anything with only one ski, so I left that one also. And I starting walking, looking for places with thin snow until I got so tired that I had to rest. I found a place under a big rock, where the wind wasn't strong, and I sat down and waited, and cried some. I thought I would die there, and Dad would come to get me. I know I sat there all night. Now and then I got up and stomped my feet, when they got really cold. And when I woke up, I knew that I couldn't go anywhere without my skis, and they were gone. And so I just sat there. It wasn't so cold, because I had the sun, at least most of the day.

Then it got colder, when it was shade. I kept falling asleep. I woke up when I heard you calling me. I saw you chugging up the slope to my big rock, shouting. I thought it was Dad, and that I had died and we were in heaven. Then I saw your cap, and I knew that my Dad would never wear anything as goofy as that. And when you came up to me, and said, 'Missy, I've come to take you home!' I could see that you weren't Dad, and I understood what was happening."

"You gave me a fright. I wasn't sure you were alive."

"Hamlin, there is something that I don't understand. Why were you calling me Missy? The reports must have given my real name. How did you know to call me Missy? It's my nickname that my Dad started, that everyone calls me. But how did you know? And you kept calling me that in the hut!"

Everything stopped. I had just been whacked on the head with a small bat swung by a tiny angel. Am I going mad? I hadn't heard her name on the weather radio; of course I would have remembered that. It was only a "twelve year-old girl," then a "twelve year-old cross-country skier." There was no name.

Ok. Ok. Ok! Enough of the angels. There is a rational explanation. I had been cruising along, wishing I had a bell or horn or something, and calling, "Miss! Miss!" because I didn't know her name. Then I thought that it sounded as though I were looking for a waitress. So I started calling "Missy" – it's more euphonious and easier to repeat. Is that the answer? Or am I afraid to accept the fact of the presence of the angels in our lives, and looking for a way to explain them away? We can account for just so much by coincidence, but her *name*? Out of the hundreds possible? Look at a topographic map of the quadrangles including the lift area and the hut, and ask a statistics major at the U to figure the odds of a random searcher spotting one small person. Then look at a book of girls' names and nicknames, and count the odds of picking the right one. Then multiply the two to get the probability of getting both right at the same time. No, the angel who showed me where she was, also told me her name. I know this. And that is what I told Missy.

She accepted this for now, and would work it all out later. But she was looking at me, worried. She misunderstood my silent, pensive frowning.

"Now you know that I really am the reason you went to prison."

"No, Missy, you are not the reason. Your parents and the CPS and the Sheriff's Department and the prosecutors and lots of other people are the reason."

"But if I hadn't run away, it wouldn't have happened!" She was choking and her voice trembling. "And you wouldn't have lost your family, and your business and everything!"

"And I wouldn't have you now."

In balance, I thought, I have more now than I had when I went up the mountain. I guess the only big loss, and irretrievable, was the company of my boys. Everything else can be caught up. I can live five years longer in the company of this wonderful lady, and I am recovering my financial losses.

"Do you mean that what I told you doesn't change things?"

That's it? That's all?

A big gust of wind blew off Bellingham Bay, scattering leaves over the table and us, and sticking one on her right cheek. She absently brushed it away, her eyes still on mine. All the clouds and confusion in my mind had been blown away, and there was left only a young woman looking at me across the wide table, waiting for an answer to her important question.

"Things?" I said. "Missy, there are no 'things.' There are only you and I. Everything else is only stuff." I waited, and watched her look at me. Her lips trembled, and she shifted a bit on the bench; she took a deep breath and tried to speak but could not.

"Missy, when I said that I love you, I meant unconditionally and forever." Her eyes filled with tears so fast that I was alarmed. Her face plopped down on her folded arms on the table, and she started waves of great, heaving sobs. She was bawling like a baby.

A woman passerby asked, "Are you all right, Miss?"

I extricated myself from my bench, crossed over, and straddled her bench, next to her. I put my arm across her shoulder, leaned close, and said "Do you understand that I love you, and you alone, always?" I kissed a bundle of red curls, as there was no other place accessible to kiss.

After a while, she sat up and looked at the table with her hair-stuck, messy face, and opened her mouth, but couldn't speak. I got out a clean hankie, turned her around, and wiped her eyes and face.

"Let's go. Will you show me that ring store?"

And after a few moments of tidying up, we walked away, her arms hugging one of mine, with not a few concerned people watching, back to the Whatcom Home Security van. And then to the ring store.

✳   ✳   ✳

One day, we were married at the small greystone church that was above a long and wide green lawn sloping down to Bellingham Bay.

Only the people who were close to us were there: Felix and Frieda; Abe and his new wife Charlotte; Ray and Nancy; Lee and Sherry. We had invited Missy's mother and stepfather at my request; Missy had said that they wouldn't come, and they didn't. Claire and Arthur, and my boys, were in school.

Nancy and Charlotte had helped Missy get ready. And when I saw her, a lump rose in my throat as I saw God's most beautiful creation, red ringlets around her face that crowned the white dress that she was entitled to wear.

When the minister spoke the words, there was an invisible chorus of angels in the rafters of the sanctuary exulting, "We did it!" I know because I heard them. Our love and faith had been tested for a terrible time, but neither we nor the angels had failed in the long journey from San Diego and Kirkland to the snow cave, and to the church.

*   *   *

The next morning, we lazed in bed and talked. Missy said, "Until now, I was a virgin, and I don't mean a Bill Clinton virgin. You know, when we slept together the first time, in the snow cave and the hut, I had no more thought of sex, yours or mine, than little kids watching cartoons wonder about all those animals running around with no pants on, and no gear showing! Oh, that time when I didn't have my panties on, remember? And you made me wrap up in a blanket – like a 'Tootsie Roll,' you said!" She laughed. "I was so naïve! But you were really great—you didn't make me feel embarrassed. You didn't want my bum to get cold, you said!

The second time, at the Nooksack cabin, I knew! Hey, I was eighteen, right? I wondered what would happen. I was so much in love with you, that you could have done anything! But I'm glad now that we didn't do anything, because now it is so wonderful! I know that you were right in following the angels! "

*   *   *

One day, we discussed how the whole wild adventure had started.

I remembered the course catalog from Bellevue Community College that led me to enroll in the cross-country skiing course. That started the sequence of events.

But there was something incomplete here. It went back to the catalog. I'd lived at the same address for three years. The BCC quarterly catalog had appeared only once. I had been skimming the catalog. I wasn't looking for sports, especially. What had made the skiing course, among the hundreds of offerings, attract my attention?

Most of my files had been lost in the divorce, the sale of the business, and the other assets. But I had managed to retain some of my personal files, including everything relating to my cross-country skiing, and everything subsequent. I searched through a couple of cardboard boxes of archives, and found the catalog. It was addressed to me, and had a printed mailing label, with the usual obscure numbers, looking as though it had come from an established list. Except for the front and back covers, the entire catalog was in black and white.

But on page fifty-nine, the course offering for cross-country skiing had been precisely encircled in gold.

Then Missy reminded me of her having received one issue only, of the ski magazine that led her back to me.

And it was clear that an angel had led me to Missy on the mountain.

And we thought of other incidents, too many to be a string of coincidences.

Why did I fall down on the carpet in front of Lee and Sherry? Instead of falling in front of any of a couple hundred of students and teachers in the BCC lounge, who didn't have a hut on Mt. Baker?

I didn't tell her how the angel enabled me to defeat Fulwood. Missy would never hear that part of my life.

I thought of our meeting with her mother and stepfather, and the brief fight. And how Russ had been going out the door as we came in. I couldn't have fought both of them. Had a renegade angel arranged a sleazy date for Russ? And maybe encouraged Fred to have a few drinks, giving me an edge?

And we saw the whole grand picture as though it had been orchestrated by the angels from the beginning, at BCC and at the Mt. Baker ski area where Missy had skied away, all the way to the church in Bellingham.

*   *   *

As we neared sleep one night, Missy asked her question.

"Hamlin, will you always love me?"

"No. I will stop when the glacier on Mt. Baker runs a stop sign in downtown Bellingham, and pushes over the coffee shop on the corner."

"But what will I do then?"

"Push my reset button. That gets you another thousand years."

"But where is the reset button?"

"Yours to find."

And when, after a while, she located the button, Missy earned, oh, I guess, about a gazillion years of additional entitlements.

CHAPTER NINETEEN ─────────────

ONCE OR TWICE A MONTH, Felix would invite all of us out, usually in the middle of a working day. It was almost always when we were ahead of our plan, or had landed a big commercial account. Felix was happy, and that's how we wanted him. But it wasn't so much the anticipation of a free meal; breakfast, lunch or dinner with Felix was show time.

Felix didn't have a script. But what would be sure to get the show going, was the question from a waiter or waitress, "How is your enchilada (or hamburger or whatever)?" It's the perfunctory and obligatory question that is in the Operations Manual.

Felix would reply, "Wait, I'll ask."

Then he would lean over his plate, and ask, "Enchilada, how are you?"

He would straighten up, and his mouth would not move, and he would look to the plate for an answer.

"I am very well, thank you, how are you?" the enchilada would say.

And the server would scream in surprised delight.

One time, he had French onion soup. The question was asked. He asked the soup.

In what was, I guess, a good Parisian accent, the soup said, "Monsieur, how would you be, if you were being eaten for lunch?"

And the girl would rush to get the other waitresses, and they would gather around to hear the talking soup.

But he wouldn't repeat it. The girls would cluster around the table, and

134

Felix would have a deadpan look on his face. But so that the first girl would not lose face, a plate would lift off the table a bit, and clatter down.

And someone would grab the plate and look underneath; there was nothing there.

One day, during a busy lunchtime, several waitresses were clustered around the table giggling, waiting to see the next trick. Then a stern-faced manager came to the table, and the girls scattered. He wanted to know, politely, if there was a problem here.

Felix said, "We have had a very enjoyable lunch, and hope to come back again soon. But, I must ask you to do something about your dishes."

The manager looked quizzically at Felix. Then a water glass in the middle of the table fell over. The manager's eyes became saucers, and he took several steps backward in fright.

Felix had his wallet trick, which he used on a couple of occasions in the evening. When the waiter presented the check, Felix would ask, "May I pay you?"

"Certainly, sir."

"Good," he would say, pulling a slim wallet from his hip pocket. "Because this money is just burning a hole in my pocket." And he would open the wallet, and it would burst into flames. And even though Missy and Abe and I or whoever was at the table had seen it before, just the look on the waiter's face would be enough to have all of us collapsing into silly laughing.

Felix told me once, "That one's easy. Go to a magic shop!"

When I asked him once about his skills, he dismissed my question with a wave of his hand. "Naaah, I gave up that stuff a long time ago." And Frieda just smiled when I asked her. She wouldn't tell me either. But years later, after Felix died, she confided that her late husband and Felix had been a professional team when they were young.

"They were the best!"

*   *   *

Years later, Missy was still doing this:

A large rubber mallet from my workshop would suddenly appear at Missy's table setting at dinner, as though it were an extra spoon. It had a wooden handle, about a foot long, with a cylindrical rubber end the size of a small ham.

At some point near the end of the meal, Missy would ask, "Hamlin Cross, do you love me?"

And I would go off in an exercise of obfuscation, like "The dimensions of my answer are so enormous, that I can't answer simply. It wouldn't give proper credit to your question." Or I would say something silly like "How do I love thee? Let a Cray supercomputer count the ways."

"This is a 'yes' or 'no' question, Mr. Cross!"

"But I can't do justice to your question with one word. What I feel, and will try to describe as best I can, is a love greater than…"

"Answer the question!" she would shout, hitting the big mallet on the table, making the dishes bounce and clatter.

"Yes."

And she would come over to my side of the table, and I would stand up, and we would hug until the coffee got cold.

It was like having to make a presentation before the class, when I was in grade school. I had better be ready, not knowing when I would be called upon. It could be any day, but only about once a month. I wouldn't know until I saw the mallet on the table by her place setting.

One evening, Missy held court. I had prepared a special dinner of chicken breasts sautéed in a cream sauce with morels over rice, and steamed asparagus, her favorites. There was a frizzy salad, with a light soy and sesame dressing. There was my special prune whip for dessert.

I had put a chilled bottle of Chablis on the table.

It was the wine that did it.

After we had finished the salad and entrée, she left the table for a moment, and returned with the mallet.

Uh-oh, I thought. We haven't even had dessert.

The judge slammed down the gavel. "Unless you want twenty hard years in stony lonesome, you will address the court, and you will tell the court how much you love me!"

"How many stars are in the Milky Way?"

"Trite!"

"How many grains of sand on the beach?"

"Not good enough!"

"How many beautifully colored feathers in an enchanted forest full of lovebirds?"

"Better, improving, but still not good enough! Start thinking bread and water, Mister! Lifetime!"

"How many rainbows in a million planets full of sunshine and rain?"

"You're not there yet!"

"If an infinite number of monkeys had an infinite number of PC's with word processing software, printers, connecting cables, ink cartridges, service contracts, and infinite paper, electric power and time, how many times would they write 'Hamlin loves Missy!'?"

"You have just exonerated yourself, prisoner! You may sit in that big chair over there, while I jump in your lap!"

The prune whip was forgotten.

Later, in bed, she wouldn't stop. "How many quarks in Queensland? How many electrons in Ecuador? Goats in Georgia? How many hairdryers in Honolulu? Kitchens in Kansas? Jumping beans in Jalisco?"

"Good night, Missy," I groaned.

I was soon on the edge of sleep. Totally in love, starting to dream…

"Rubles in Russia?" woke me up.

This is the last time I serve wine with dinner.

I asked "How many sweet loves in this bed?"

"Two!"

"You win! Goodnight! At least one of the two needs his sleep!"

Missy's face moved toward mine slowly, and all the silliness was gone. And I saw in the half-light the look of adoration that I had first seen in the snow cave. She touched my hair, and gave me the softest, most tender and sweetest kiss that I had ever experienced or imagined.

And then we slept as one.

CHAPTER TWENTY ━━━━━━━━━

WE BEGAN TO EXPERIENCE A startling run of false alarms – well over our average. The Bellingham Police and the Whatcom Sheriff's Department were very concerned. Our good reputation for accurate installation and careful training of our customers was being smudged. Abe, Felix and I looked at the events and saw a geographic pattern; it was as though someone were on a delivery route, going from house to house that was under our protection, and trying a door or window, then going on. Someone had our customer list - but the police and the sheriff's department had it, and the alarm monitoring company had it. And each of our protected properties had a yard sign or window decal, so our customer list was not really a secret. I thought about who might be doing this: a competitor, a potential competitor, or an extortionist. I knew our competitors, and dismissed that possibility.

The answer came during a discussion over beer, with Detective Sergeant Johnnie Morse, point man for organized crime in the county. Organized crime? In Bellingham?

"You know about the big Chinese immigration just across the border, in Vancouver. They are well-to-do, and mostly legitimate. Some of the triads, the Chinese mafia, are there too. But we haven't seen any spillover into Washington, no signs of mob activity from there. But there is a colony of recent Russian immigrants, trailer-house white trash, living east of here, toward Mt. Baker and near the border. The older ones are ok, but the younger ones generally don't work or go to school, they just steal or prostitute themselves. Most of this has just been petty, and an annoyance, but now we see signs that someone is trying to organize them; it looks like they want to go into the trash-collection and recycling business. Some of the drivers in existing companies have been intimidated, and it looks like it will get worse. It's like one city in California used to be, until the city council decided to give the mob a monopoly, to stop the killings.

Now, it looks like they may want to get into the security business. Some of their thugs have signed on as bodyguards for rich Vancouver visitors going to the tribal casinos here. But they may have discovered that there is more to the security business -- once you install an alarm system in someone's house, office, or place of business, you know the address, what valuables are there, and how to defeat the system Especially medical offices – they want the dope.

I am guessing that this is what is behind your false alarms - discredit you and present themselves as an alternative. Another possibility is that they just want to be paid off, to go away. Trouble with accepting this as a solution, is that they will keep coming back."

"Who is behind this?"

"Steve Petrov is the brains. He's easy to find."

I arranged a meeting with Petrov. I figured they would have big numbers, and only Abe and I could present ourselves. When I told Abe of the time and venue, he said that he would arrange some backup.

We met at the cheesy kind of hotel that I would have expected them to have chosen. As we walked into the suite, I flipped the night security device on the door, to keep it partly open. We were faced with a beefy Russian flanked by four lean and casually savage- looking punks. The big one introduced himself as Petrov. I knew he wasn't. He looked too stupid; he couldn't have been the brains behind a pushcart. A smaller man was standing against the wall, just watching and listening. He wore a goatee, a speedo suit and a long leather coat. He is the brains, I thought, and the one with the gun. But I knew that we might be set up, so we watched all of them.

We were facing a group of inarticulate gangsters, but I found my words wanting. What is the protocol for a meeting like this? Do you want to take over my business, or to destroy it? Or do you want to be paid off? I had no business negotiation skills. I should have taken a course. Then Fulwood strode through the door and kept walking, straight into the phalanx of Russians.

In the old days, before bowling alleys had automatic pinsetters, the job was done by pin boys. I know because I was a pin boy in my junior high-school days. Well today, I had my old job back, because Russians were flying like tenpins. I picked up the nearest flanker and threw him into the wall. But for that, anything Abe and I might have done would have been gratuitous, so we just watched. Abe was fixated on Mr. Speedo Suit, and when a gun started to show, he closed the short gap between him and Petrov as a sprinter off the block; a big fist knocked Petrov senseless, and his gun clattered onto the floor. Abe kicked it away.

I frisked each dazed and bleeding Russian. One had a knife, which I opened and broke in two. The big one was on all fours like a pig, foaming onto the floor. Fulwood watched the bunch as Abe guided each to the elevator and pushed the down button. Petrov was now sitting up against the wall, his front covered with his blood and saliva.

We held Petrov, and I punched 911. As the police took Petrov away in plastic cuffs, Fulwood turned to Abe and asked, "You said you have some work for me to do?"

I asked, "You guys hungry? I'm up for steak and potatoes."

*   *   *

We had a new alarm installer, Cynthia Cisneros. Cynthia ("*never* Cindy!") was an early-twenties woman, a graduate of a vocational school with a two-year curriculum in electronics and alarm installation. She was just slightly plump, and had buck teeth that shone through an ever-ready and beautiful smile.

One day, Cynthia was driving to a residential alarm installation, when her van was forced off the road. The assailant had seen that there was no one riding shotgun; it hadn't occurred to him that someone might be in the windowless back. Cynthia was pulled from her driver's seat.

A police investigator told me later that he had seen road accidents in which a pedestrian had been knocked through the windshield of the striking vehicle, and he had seen cases in which unbelted drivers and passengers had been thrown through their windshields. But he had never before seen a case in which a driver had entered his *own* vehicle through the windshield.

It was the damndest thing, he told me. "I just can't figure these Russians!"

We kept up our watch, but we had no more trouble from the mob.

CHAPTER TWENTY-ONE ————

THERE WAS A VOICEMAIL MESSAGE from Ray—"Urgent, please call." I phoned him at home.

"I've got good news for you, Hamlin. Can we meet at my office at nine, tomorrow morning? Missy also?"

"So?"

"You'll never knock on doors again, Hamlin."

The next morning, Missy and I faced Ray across his desk. It had folding legs, like the tables in the school lunchroom.

"Let me give you the background. You know that we have filed a suit against the County. And the State, because of the CPS involvement. They have responded jointly.

Both of you have massive, popular support, by virtue of your story—the reversals of the convictions. Your personal story, too, Missy." We knew that it had already been picked up by the teen magazines, even in Japan. Missy had made a huge montage out of the articles.

"The greens love you — you're skiers. Not only that, but you're cross-country skiers. You don't defile anything. You're like Indians on snowshoes. No ski lifts, no humongous lodges. You don't stay in lodges, do you?" Ray was having his fun. "I don't know where we would be if you were snowmobilers, though... The civil libertarians love you — you're innocents who were savaged by an out-of-control state agency, and bad-guy prosecutors. The law and order, NRA people are with you; they are not always with the government, since Waco and Idaho. The loggers haven't taken a position, but I don't see a worry there. Everybody loves you guys!" Ray's eyes were shining. I'd never seen him like this.

"Well, the governor looks at this suit, and sees disaster. Someone will write a book about it. Maybe make a movie! It's cut and dried. Everybody can understand. There's no ambiguity. There's the very dramatic reversal of your convictions." He waited for a moment. "The governor doesn't need this. He's facing reelection. The whole thing could sink him. Olympia is where the buck stops, not Bellingham. Everyone will want to know why he hasn't cleaned up the agency. Anyway, it all means that we have them by the short"—he paused, remembering Missy's presence—"I mean we have them …."

"By the balls?" Missy offered. Ray laughed. I'd never seen Ray laugh before.

"Well. What it comes down to, is that I have met with the State and the County, as I told you." Ray stopped for a moment, and seemed to go inside himself for a while. Then, "We worked out the numbers. I can show you, if you want," he said, gesturing toward a thick folder. "So much for your lost income, which partially offsets the fair market value for SOUND Home Security as an ongoing business, minus the distress sale price that you actually got, plus five years' interest. So much additional for loss of liberty, loss of reputation, pain and suffering, for both." He nodded toward Missy.

"Are you ready?" He stopped for a while, and then looked at one paper. "Here's what it comes to. The offer is a round $3 million for you, $1 million for Mrs. Cross. Plus legal fees, meaning my fees and expenses. Out of the $4 million, I get one-third, per our agreement." He sat back to let it all sink in. We sipped on our coffee.

"We can go for a jury trial and maybe get more. I think we should settle, now. I don't think you want to get back on the stand in front of those ugly people, or wait months or years if they appeal. They know we are thinking jury, and that's why they came up with a reasonable number quickly. But the State is politics, and things could change. If the governor is voted out, and there is a protracted appeal process, his successor would see no advantage to closing quickly. Blame it on the last guy."

I looked at Missy. She nodded. "Let's do it," I said.

"I'll have papers to sign this week, and we'll have the checks within sixty days."

Ray relaxed, breathing very deeply, several times. He seemed to be somewhere else, for a few moments. Then, "So, what are you going to do with the money?" His face was flushed. He was trying hard to make small talk.

"Well, I guess we can finish the cabin, right?" I said, turning to Missy.

"Don't forget the new fridge," she cautioned.

"How about you, Ray?" I asked.

"Me? I'm going to take up cross-country skiing, now that I see how much money there is in it! Don't forget, yours is tax-free. I have to pay taxes on mine."

"Would it cheer you up if we invited you and Nancy to dinner on Friday? We'll pay two-thirds!"

Ray started laughing at this, and couldn't stop. He kept going. He doubled over in his chair, his shoulders heaving. It was Missy who first understood that he was crying, and went to his side with her arms across his shoulders.

Then I realized that I really didn't know this man at all. I knew that he had come from the East Coast after leaving law school and then his military service, with his college sweetheart, years ago. And that they were still in a rented apartment and were running a family law office in one room over a vacuum cleaner repair shop. I thought of the car that they drove. And that his days were filled with pro bono work from the prisons and welfare offices, and fed by student advocate groups. And that Nancy was still a substitute public school teacher.

His strain over the past weeks hadn't been apparent. He was always cocky, self-sure, almost arrogant. He had been hiding his need to make the great triumph, the big score, to affirm his competence and to show Nancy and the world that he was a lawyer with the best of them. His defeating the County prosecutors in high-profile cases had put him on the map. But now, he was no longer honored by only the losers in life; he was not just a folk hero with the students. Now everyone would know who he was. He had just defeated the State of Washington. Everyone would know the numbers, the money. Maybe not much in New York, but pretty visible in Bellingham and Olympia.

When he got up, I turned away for a while to let him collect himself. Then I went back to both, for a great three-way hug.

"You're on for Friday!" Ray said.

* * *

We bought out Frieda. That was what she and Felix wanted, and had expected would happen someday; the settlement made it possible today, no terms. Felix no longer had to stay to help his brother's widow; she was now financially independent.

Felix said, "I didn't like the business anyway!" He owned an upscale motel in Arizona, and was ready to get back to his golfing. "Anything that gets in the way of golf, I don't need! This is not golf country! Arizona, Florida, North Carolina, yes! If I could play St. Andrews every week, I'd move to Scotland. Even if the weather is even worse than here!"

We settled on a fair price; the name and customer base were worth something, but other than that, only Abe and I added value. The deal was good for all of us.

Frieda stayed on as bookkeeper; she was happy to continue what she had been doing. This was her home. Her husband was buried here and their children and grandchildren were not far away. Bellingham and Whatcom Home Security were what she knew, and she was happy.

Chapter Twenty-two ——————

I WAS ALONE IN THE office, at about four in the afternoon, when the phone rang. It was Missy.

"Hamlin, Claire called me. Russ is in Bellingham."

"Why?"

"He plays football for San Diego State—they're playing WWU tomorrow. An exhibition game. He's a linebacker or something. He dropped hints to his friends about

'a second agenda' in Bellingham. He told someone he was 'going to kick ass twice.' Claire picked this up from her friends. Hamlin, he's mean, like his father. Watch out for him."

"Missy, you keep the door locked. Don't let him in if he comes there. Call me if he does. See you at six."

An hour later, I was still alone in the office. Abe was out on an alarm installation, and I was doing some paperwork. Frieda had taken the day off to be with her grandchildren.

I saw what looked like a big rental sedan pull up outside. It was listing to one side. Two large men got out. I recognized Russ. The other was sized like a freezer; when he got out, the car righted itself. While I waited for them to come up the stairs and inside, I pressed two buttons under the desk, and opened a drawer. I took my weapon out, released the safety, and put it in a pocket of my cargo pants. They walked up the stairs, and inside.

The two framed themselves in front of my desk. "What's up, guys?"

"You sucker-punched my dad. I thought we might talk about it," said Russ.

"Both of you?"

"Maybe I like having a witness, in case you pull some shit on me, like you did on my dad."

"Well, you know, that's not how I remember it. Your mom and Missy were there. Do they agree that I sucker-punched him?" I was smoking him out. I knew that he and Missy did not communicate.

"Missy!" He tried to put a contemptuous look on his face. "Do you think I'd listen to anything that fucking slut said?"

I had hoped to end this peaceably. But one last try for peace.

"Well, let me show you guys out. I'm really not into beating up kids."

They laughed.

"Ok, guys. Both of you out the door. Or do I call the police?"

"I can beat the shit out of you before you can reach the phone."

I sighed in resignation. "Ok, but let's move this outside."

The big kid sneered, "Sure, we wouldn't want to mess up your really classy office." That hurt. The office hadn't been done by a decorator, but I thought it was ok. And Frieda put in fresh flowers regularly.

"I'm sorry you don't like it," I said. "By the way, we haven't been introduced. My name's Hamlin. What's yours?"

"Why is that any of your fucking business?"

"I need a name to give to the ambulance attendants."

They laughed again. "His name is Dexter, and he kicks ass," said Russ. "So watch your mouth."

"Well, gentlemen, after you" I said, gesturing toward the door. They went out the door, and down the steps to the parking lot. I followed them a few steps behind.

They reached the bottom of the stairs, and then stood side by side, waiting for me. I stepped quickly to the left side of the bigger one. "This is for you, Dexter," I said as I gave him a full blast of the bear spray in his huge face. Now, bear spray has much the same formulation as people spray, oleoresin capsicum, or OC, but it comes in a larger container and has a wider aperture. The reason for this is that bears, especially grizzlies, tend to be larger than people, and they need more of the product, and faster, to stop them.

Dexter's hands went to his face, and he screamed, as his eyes, nostrils and lips caught fire. I like to be remembered by people whom I meet for the first time, so I gave him a smart snap kick at the place where his massive thighs joined. The scream dropped half an octave, like the Doppler effect of the whistle of a train as it goes by. Dexter was down.

Russ had unavoidably caught a whiff of the spray and had backed away. Then he was facing me, assuming what he thought was a boxer's stance. I pushed the spray canister back into my pocket. Russ was too good for bear spray.

I stepped in and hit him once in his mouth with my left, splitting his lower lip. "First blood wins the fight," Abe had said.

"Hold it!" I said, putting up both palms. Russ backed off a bit, holding his mouth. "When is the big game?" I asked.

"What?"

"The game! When?"

"Tomorrow!"

"Russ, would you like to play in the game, or would you like to watch it on tape from your hospital bed a month from now? Those are your two options."

He stood for a while, trying hard to decide. Then he turned to Dexter, who was sitting on the gravel, wheezing, his eyes still slammed shut and tearing. His face was red and puffy, and he was probably wishing he had been born a girl.

"Let's go back to the hotel, Dexter," Russ said. He passed in front of me to go to his friend.

Stupidity runs through that family as the Mississippi runs through Memphis. Did he really believe that I would fall for this?

As he passed, he spun around with a savage overhand right. I ducked it, and hit him hard in his solar plexus. He crouched, waiting for his breath to return.

Suddenly I heard the crying voice of Missy, saying fix him, Hamlin, so he can't touch me again, please, Hamlin! And that's when everything fell into place.

Clunk.

One. When Missy first told me about her stepfather, Russ's father, physically abusing her, I had asked, "Did he molest you?" We had been distracted for a moment, and she had asked "Who?" Now I understood.

Two. When Russ and Missy had briefly met at their parents' hotel a few months ago, not a word nor a glance had passed between them, though they had grown up together.

Three. He had just referred to her in vile obscenities.

Hamlin, the developmentally-challenged child, had just put together a three-piece jigsaw puzzle, all by himself!

Now I was ready to go to work. For my Missy. But Russ, this will also be for every kid that you bullied from kindergarten on, for every girl you insulted or raped, for every person you gave injury and pain to, with your big body and slimy urges. I knew Russ. Everyone knows Russ. The rage welled up from every part of my body and mind. I thought of this thug, this piece of filth, passing his genes into the human pool, and was appalled by what I saw.

My work was methodical. Every punch had all my practice behind it, and was part of a plan to create a mosaic of facial injuries for lifetime viewing. I was the makeup man, today. But I stayed away from the brainpan. I wanted him on his feet. I had big plans for Russ. Did you really refer to my dear wife as a "fucking slut"?

The guys who work on the decks of aircraft carriers know the rule: you never step *over* a cable, you step *on* it. If a cable unexpectedly springs up from the deck, you will be tossed for a loop, but with your protective headgear, you will get through okay, maybe with some injuries. But if you step *over* it, it will take the surgeons a week to find just where in your body your testicles have become lodged.

An F-14 whooshed out of the sky, and approached the deck for a landing. It touched, tires screeched and smoked, and it bounced and came down again. The cables snagged the undercarriage of the big plane. Just as Russ stepped *over* the cable.

I hope I never hear a scream like that again. On the other hand, I wish I could have recorded it for Missy.

After he had exhausted his lungs, Russ lay on the ground in a partial fetal position, his hands between his legs, his bloody face framing a mouth wide open in a silent cry.

Every now and then, when I critique my life, and I think of the successes and failures, I think that, in balance, I have accounted well for myself. But I also think of the things that have been done well, that might have been done better. And I wonder if I couldn't have kicked Russ just a little bit harder.

A Whatcom Home Security van sped into the lot and skidded to a stop, spraying gravel. A Bellingham Police black-and-white was directly behind it, flashers on. Abe jumped out, looked at the scene, walked over and said nothing, but put a hand on my arm. I found out later that Missy had paged him, and had asked him to look out for me.

Two officers got out of the car, and walked over. They understood why Abe had been speeding, and let it go. "You did this?"

"Yes. I'm Hamlin Cross. This is my company. Mr. Lincoln, here, is on my staff." We were both in our company uniforms.

"Can you tell me what happened?"

"They are football players from San Diego, and came over here to beat me up. I gave the big one some OC," I said, handing him the can of bear spray. "Then I kicked him in the balls." He was taking notes. "That one," I said, pointing, "I punched several times, and also kicked him in the balls. They will need attention. I haven't called for medical help yet because it just finished."

"They'll get attention, all right," he said. He was a WWU fan, I guessed. The other officer was on his radio. Then I told him why the football players wanted to beat me up.

"We'll stay until the ambulance comes. You'll have to make a statement. We will meet them at the hospital and put a hold on them. I guess you'll want to press charges."

"Yes." I handed him my business card.

After the ambulance arrived and left, listing to one side, the police left also. As they went to their cruiser, one turned and tossed me the can of bear spray. "This is yours," he said. "Watch out for those bears!" And I think that they imagined, when they looked at Abe, what Russ and Dexter would look like if he had been here also.

I replied, "Don't bet on San Diego tomorrow!" They laughed.

I finished my paperwork, and was home for dinner at six, as promised.

Chapter Twenty-three ——————

When Missy didn't have an evening class, she always greeted me at the door with a big hug. I got my hug, but there was something missing. She squeezed me harder than usual, but she wasn't really there.

She knew that something had happened — maybe she saw it in my eyes?

"You fixed him, didn't you?"

"He won't touch you again, Missy."

She wasn't surprised at what I said. But she looked as though her past had caught up with her.

Dinner could wait. "I'll tell you what happened today, if you'll tell me about you and Russ."

We sat down on the two big chairs that face the fireplace, and I told her briefly what had happened to Russ today. And then she started her story.

"One night when Mom and Fred were out, he and some buddies were drinking beer downstairs, and watching TV. They were pretty boisterous. They were the same bunch of rough guys, bullies, that he ran with at high school. I was in my jammies, and I didn't want to go to the kitchen, even with a robe on. After a while, they left. I didn't hear anything for a while, and I didn't know if he had left with them or not. I always kept my door locked, and I checked it to be sure.

I still felt funny. I had a nice red pocketknife that Arthur had given me for my fifteenth birthday, a week before. I thought it was kind of a goofy present, from a boy to a girl, but it was Arthur's present, so I cherished it.

Claire had given me a framed photo of the three of us - that one - " she said pointing to the silver- framed photo on the mantle. I had looked at it often; it was the picture of the three friends, which Missy had shown me at the Nooksack cabin.

"Well, I loved those presents. And I kept them under my pillow. Now, I was afraid, and I went to my bed, and opened the big blade on the knife, and put it back under the pillow.

A while later, I went down to the kitchen to get some milk. I didn't see him. But when I came back to my room, he was there, looking at stuff on my desk. He never came in my room; he knew that he was not welcome there. I was scared because he was there, and no one else was home. I told him that I was studying, and please go to your own room.

"Who do you think you are, a fucking princess?" "Get out!" I shouted back. He jerked on my bathrobe belt, untying it. Then he picked me up and threw me on my bed. I was screaming and crying. I tried to hit his face, and he slapped me. He got my robe off, and started working on my jammies. He pulled the cord on my bottoms, and started pulling them down. I knew that the only way to stop him was to get the knife. I was glad that I had opened the blade. But he saw what I was doing and grabbed my wrist, took the knife away, and tossed it on the bed behind him.

He had my bottoms over my knees, and was starting on my panties. I was crying hysterically, but I still knew that I would not let him rape me, no matter what. I might be able to reach the knife. So I still pretended to struggle, and he got my panties over my knees, too, then pulled everything over my ankles. Then I sat up to him, and he was looking at what he wanted and touching, and I reached, but I still couldn't reach the knife. And I lay back down, really crying, while he got ready. Then I remembered the picture. And while he was busy with his clothing, I reached under the pillow and took out the silver picture frame. He saw it, and didn't understand what I planned to do. I held it in both hands, turned on my left side a bit, then sliced it across his face, aiming for his eyes, in a backhand with all the strength I had. And it cut across his cheek and his nose, and blood spurted out. He screamed, "you fucking bitch!" and grabbed my throat and tried to choke me.

Just then Claire and Arthur came through the door. They had just walked in the front door as they always did; they saw my light from the street and knew I would be studying. They heard me screaming and crying, and ran up to my room. They stood for a second, then moved.

Well, they had been in my room so many times that they knew everything about it, including the fact that the bed posts were removable, just a male-female dowel joint, unglued, to make it easier to move, I guess. One goofy afternoon, we tried to play pickup sticks with them. Anyway, Claire quickly pulled off one post from the foot of the bed and handed it to Arthur as though they had rehearsed this. Arthur looked at it for a second. Then he shouldered it and whacked it so hard across the back of Russ' head that I thought he'd killed him. Russ fell forward on me with all his blood, and started foaming at his mouth even before Arthur and Claire could drag him off me, and drop him on the floor.

Then Claire pulled me up, and into the bathroom. I sat on the toilet seat crying while she ran the shower for me, and then she helped me to clean up. She found some clean panties and jammies for me, while Arthur stood guard over Russ, still holding the bedpost. The funny thing is that I didn't mind Arthur seeing me naked. He didn't look, but he couldn't help having seen me.

Then we heard some sounds downstairs, and Arthur went to the door and called down, 'Mr. and Mrs. Deloitte, you'd better come up here.' It wasn't a pretty sight. Mom threw up on my rug.

I got dressed and went to stay with Claire that night.

Anyway, they got Russ to the hospital, and they made up a story about an accident at home. The emergency room doctor wouldn't buy it, and reported it to the police. The gash and the concussion, all those stitches on his face and the back of his head, could not have been an accident. Somehow, it was settled, since there was no complaint. Fred has influence with the city. There was no report of an intruder, and no one was at home except his little sister.

Mom and Fred were unusually contrite. They *asked* me to never mention this. I thought sure I would get some blame for this, but no. I thought he should go to jail, and told them so. 'Don't ruin his life, Missy', my mom said. 'He made a terrible mistake.' Like he got caught peeking in the girls' locker room, or something. I told them to tell Russ that if he or any of his friends even touched Arthur, I would hold a press conference. And I meant it. For once, Fred had nothing to say. I asked Arthur and Claire not to tell anyone, and they agreed.

I wrote four identical letters with all the details, and sealed them and gave them to Claire and Arthur. I told them that if I disappeared or died, they should take the letters to the newspaper and the police. You are the first person outside the six in that room to know how Russ got that scar.

At first, my Mom wanted me to see a therapist, but she didn't push it because I would have to tell the story. So for days after that, Arthur and Claire gave up their after-school clubs and came over, and all of us would lie on my bed and talk and hug, because for a few days I couldn't stop shaking and crying. I really loved them for that. And then I was ok."

As Missy finished her story, I was filled with a feeling of gratitude that she loved and was really loved by someone other than me. Arthur and Claire and their parents were her real family, I thought; that's how she was able to survive living in that house full of horrors. And I suddenly felt a swell of affection for the skinny kid in the photo who had taken a bedpost to the big subhuman who was trying to rape his friend. If Arthur had been in front of me now, I would have hugged him until he couldn't breathe.

"But why didn't you tell me this before?"

"Because I knew you would go to San Diego and get into trouble. I just wanted to forget it, to make it go away."

Missy looked at me blankly. She had lost something.

"Missy, a bad thing happened that was not your fault. You fixed it. It came back again today. I fixed it for good. Russ is history."

Then I realized that Missy was hurt because Russ had seen and touched her. I remembered that she had said proudly, "I was a virgin, and I don't mean a Bill Clinton virgin." Exposing herself was like heavy petting or something; she was no longer technically pure, she thought. Russ had seen her private parts and had touched her long before her husband had. And she acknowledged that she let him take her panties off, so that she could distract him long enough to reach the knife. She had failed, so had lost what was precious to her, for nothing.

The fact that she had then defeated him by slashing his face with the picture frame, leaving him scarred for life, wasn't exoneration. She should have used the picture frame before she lost her panties. She too, was scarred for life.

This is what I knew Missy was thinking, and I didn't know what to do.

"Hamlin, this was very private to me. You slept with me for three nights in the snow cave and the hut, and later for a week in the Nooksack cabin, and you didn't once touch me or see me, but you still went to prison. He saw me and touched me and nothing happened to him. I lived for three years with that, living in the same house with him, and I still was ok. Until you knew about it. And now you know about it."

"Missy, it only bothers me because it bothers you. I'll take you to Japan, and we'll stay in a lodge at a hot spring, where whole families, and young couples and strangers soak in the water, with nothing on. They usually put a small towel on the right spot, but everyone can see everyone, and no one looks."

"That's different!"

She was right. Nice try. But how can I get Missy to believe that what happened was utterly insignificant to our relationship? Well, she will get more hugs, kisses, and simple touches than usual, for sure.

Missy said, "I can see in your eyes that things are different."

"Missy, do you remember in the park, before we went to the ring store, what I told you about 'things'? They don't exist for us. What you see in my eyes is my admiration for my girl who, at the age of fifteen, beat a rapist twice her size, and left the evidence on his face for the world to see as long as he lives. I didn't know that before tonight. Second, what you see is my concern that you believe that what he did somehow diminishes you. That's all there is. There is nothing that has come between us. And there is nothing that ever will."

But in bed, she was another person. We hugged tightly, but she was like cardboard. I wanted my Missy back.

We didn't see or hear the eleven-clock news item on Channel Two:

"Two San Diego players, Russ Deloitte, linebacker, and Dexter Peterson, center, were arrested for aggravated assault this afternoon after an altercation in Bellingham. Both were hospitalized with facial and other undisclosed injuries. Charges were brought by Hamlin Cross, a local businessman. Mr. Cross was uninjured, and was not charged. A police spokesman declined to identify the other participants in the brawl, but stated that no further arrests were expected."

I awoke about seven, and Missy wasn't in our bed. The bathroom light was out. Then I heard sounds downstairs, as though she were making coffee, getting breakfast ready, earlier than usual. We always did this together. I fell asleep for a few minutes, then woke up. Downstairs was silent. I went down, and saw Missy in her pajamas and robe, with a cup of coffee, staring at the table. She was embarrassed for me to see her this way. I walked behind her chair, put my arms around her, and kissed her cheek. She was still frozen. "I'll get the newspaper," she said, standing up. She went outside. I went back upstairs, and back to bed for a while. I didn't know what to do.

Later, my face was covered with shaving cream, and I had scraped off whiskers on only half of my face. I heard the fast thumping of feet on the stairs, and waited, worried, as Missy rushed into the bathroom. "Hamlin! Look! It's on the front page!" And she dropped the newspaper, and grabbed my face, and kissed me through the lather, and hugged me tight, and she was laughing and teary too. She took my hand and pulled me from the bathroom. And then both our faces were smeared with lather, and we didn't care. And I didn't care if I was late for work.

Later, she told me, "When I got the newspaper, I saw the article, and read it a few times, and I felt so proud and so grateful. I knew that you could have made Russ go away if you wanted, and you had no reason to really hurt him. But you didn't know then. But you *understood*! And you did it for me! I know that! You put him in the hospital for what he did to me!"

"So did you, Missy, and you were only fifteen!"

"But you were fighting *two* of them! You didn't tell me that! And then it was eight o'clock, and I turned on the news. Because of the game today, it was big news, so it was on right away. And they gave the same report as in the newspaper, except that she said that the police had not identified the other participants in the fight, like they were looking for ten more guys! And I knew again how big and great you are, that you beat them for *me*! They had nothing to do with your life! And when I heard that, I thought of the other great people in my life, my Dad, and Arthur and Claire, and I ran to the mantle and pulled down all their pictures, and I cried over so many people who love me and help me, and that's when the bad feeling was over. And that's when I ran to the bathroom and attacked you."

I had an idea. "Let's invite Claire and Arthur to stay with us, next school vacation?"

"Yes! Can we do that?" Her face was a burst of joy.

Then Ray phoned. "Did you know you're in the paper? And on Channel 2 news? We need to talk about this!"

"I'll call you back, Ray," I said.

I phoned Ray later in the day, and filled him in. He was still worried. "It's over," I told him.

Ray had a good sense about these things. "It's not over."

*   *   *

He called me a week later.

The parents of both kids were behind a civil suit against me. They had engaged a local attorney, whom Ray knew, and he had sounded Ray out on this over lunch or something. The approach was that I was an ex-con and an experienced street fighter, who had overreacted in a contentious situation that I could have walked away from. They said that I had invited them outside to fight. They were claiming permanent physical damage to their reproductive parts. "They know about the settlement from the State, and they want to get their hands on it."

156

"Ray, let me give you a few things to take back to your friend, and save all of us some time and trouble.

One. They sought me out; I didn't go looking for them. They came to my office; I didn't go to San Diego or to their hotel in Bellingham. No judge or jury would believe that this was a social call.

Two. I have an audio and video surveillance system in my office, which I use for demonstration purposes. I'm in the business, right? I turned it on when I saw them coming. We are all on tape, at least the indoor part. They clearly threatened to beat me up, and I clearly told them to leave. I threatened to call the police. I tried to avoid a physical confrontation. I will give you copies of these tapes, which you may share with your friend, if you wish.

Three. I don't carry a gun, though I am licensed. I had only the pepper spray, which is a legal and non-lethal defensive weapon. I could not use it indoors, or I would have gassed myself. I had to move the confrontation outside. I had no choice.

Four. I am thirty-two, and work in a sedentary occupation. They are twenty-one and twenty-two respectively, and athletes in the prime of health, and fitness." I didn't mention my jogging and regular workouts with Abe.

"Five. Together they weigh three times what I do.

Six. There is stuff on that tape, Russ's words, that would embarrass his family. His father's a big shot in San Diego, and would not want that publicity."

"Hamlin, you explain things so nicely. I think that our problem just went away."

And it did.

Chapter Twenty-four ———

There was a small cross-border gang operating in San Diego County and Baja California; they were one of many engaged in smuggling people and dope, and murder-for-hire. The latter service was made available mostly to competing drug factions in Mexico. The killings generally stopped at the border, but the San Diego City and County authorities were starting to see blood in California, as far north as Los Angeles; the gang had alliances there and in Texas border cities. There was a small task force in the San Diego County Sheriff's Department, working with the City police and Baja California authorities, to track their activities.

An informant within the gang had let it slip that two of their people had a Bellingham, Washington assignment next week. This was a first. It was just an incidental piece of information that would have just been passed on routinely to Bellingham authorities. But the informee had fastened on this. Detective Oskar Morales followed gang activities, and saw this as out of pattern. He phoned his counterpart in Bellingham. He was told, "No, we don't see that kind of thing here. I don't see anything. They don't come up here. The Mexicans are not a big part of the drug scene here – this isn't Los Angeles. Your thing must be something else."

But what?

Morales must have had an elephantine memory, and the imagination of a wizard. Bellingham? Bellingham? It's not on anyone's map here. Then it came to him. About seven years ago, a local big shot, owner of a stock brokerage, had accused a Bellingham man of kidnapping and molesting his pre-teen stepdaughter, and the guy went to prison. And a little over a year ago, she had run away from home on the eve of her high-school graduation to testify in a re-opening of the case in Bellingham, exonerating the man. And had not returned. Her stepfather was enraged – he claimed she had been brainwashed and seduced, and was being held against her will. He had tried to get the authorities to act on this, to no avail. Morales's informant was unable to make a connection between his boss and Fred Deloitte. But Morales started to see a possible picture, and it was more than anything else he had. He went back to the Bellingham police, then phoned me to tell me what he knew, and what he guessed.

I thought of the two escalating and violent attempts on me by Fred Deloitte and his son, and thought that he might want to try again, this time by proxy, and terminally. I remembered the case in Seattle in which a federal prosecutor was murdered as he worked at his home desk at night. He had presented a clear target for the hit man, who could see him clearly through the window. I figured I was up against low-quality hoods, whose imagination couldn't extend beyond finding an easy opportunity like that. But we kept up our guard for car bombs and other things, and always kept a 360-degree watch. Fulwood was Missy's constant but inconspicuous companion.

We set them up. I often worked at the office late at night. There was a high embankment behind our office, and someone at the top, in a neighbor's back yard, would have a clear shot at my back and head. Cynthia shopped for a mannequin – the only one she could find in one day was a woman, so we had to put her on a cushion and fill her out with lots of newspaper and strapping tape; Cynthia and Charlotte did something with her hair. The final result was a really convincing stage set – we checked it from the neighbor's yard. Seen through the curtains, it was an indistinct Hamlin, hunched over his desk, his back to the window. I put an oscillating fan on the floor, and a couple of sheaves of paper tacked to the desk by one corner: the fan lifted the papers intermittently, giving the illusion that I was shuffling papers. I continued to work at night – my van missing from the parking area would have been a giveaway. But I moved to an out-of-sight desk. Abe stood watch in our unmarked van on the upper street.

One night that week as I worked, our beautiful mannequin jerked into the desk, then slumped and fell as three booming shots rang out and the wall opposite my desk splintered. I waited. I knew Abe would have been watching as soon as he saw the hit man enter the neighbor's yard. So I just sat and waited.

I heard a clunk – thump – clunk -- as though something heavy were being pulled up the stairs. I opened the door. Abe stepped in, dragging the hit man as a terrier would drag in a rat. A rifle was in his other hand.

"Dude's been in an accident. It's so bad that he can't remember where he works."

We waited until he was conscious, then Abe propped him up in a chair in front of my desk, away from the window. Abe had to straighten him now and then, as he leaned near the floor. I gave him some moistened wipes to clean his blood-messed face. Abe had checked him all over – he had no identification, nothing in his pockets. He had been dropped off quickly in a fast-moving car with no lights.

I knew that the car would have come back quickly to pick him up, and that when they did not see him, they would have understood that something had gone wrong. He had a two-way radio that Abe had pocketed. They would not stick around. I phoned the police, out of the earshot of Hit Man. I knew that I had some time to work with.

I wrote out a script. "I understand that this interview is being recorded, and I give my consent." This statement is required under federal and state law, in order for a recording to be admissible in court. I didn't think the tape could be used as evidence anyway, but I wanted to know the answers.

This was not playtime. I was looking at a thing who had just tried to put three big slugs through my head and back. I thought of what I ought to do. I was in the position of a potential torturer, like police or military, wherever in the world. This animal had just tried to kill the person whom Missy loved most. Imagining her grief kindled enough rage to make me want to rip this thing into bite-sized pieces of dog food. But an angel was watching, and she let me know that she was watching.

"Are you going to answer my questions?" He looked at me blankly. "Abe, get the water jug." Abe was behind the guy, and gave me a questioning look. "The big one, and the rubber face mask and two of the plastic tubes, too. And the bicycle pump." Neither Abe nor I had any idea as to how we would conduct torture with this apparatus, even if we had it, but the possibilities that presented themselves apparently occurred to Mr. Hit Man at the same time. Abe dropped a five-gallon water jug next to the guy's chair, then turned and pretended to assemble the other gear. The hit man's face turned white; his eyes looked like bottle caps.

"Simon Marcos pays me."

"That's not what I asked you, asshole. I asked you if you are going to answer my questions."

"Yes."

I turned on the recorder, and handed him the script. He read it aloud. Then I began:

"What is your name?"

"Narciso Redmond."

"Where do you live?"

"xxx y Street, National City, California."

"Why are you in Bellingham?"

A pause. "Are you Hamlin Cross?"

"I ask the questions. You answer them."

"I am here to kill Hamlin Cross."

"Who paid you to kill him?"

"Simon Marcos pays me."

I thrust a finger into his chest. "I asked you who paid you to kill *him*!"

A short pause. "Simon Marcos!"

"Who paid *him*?"

"I don't know!"

There was no reason not to believe him, and I really didn't want to go through the water torture charade again.

The police arrived, measurements and photos were taken and Abe and I were questioned. Narciso and his rifle were taken away.

One of the officers was the senior of the pair who had picked up Russ and Dexter. "You have trouble making friends, don't you?"

The evidence was all over the place. Narciso was prosecuted, convicted of attempted murder, and sentenced to fifteen years imprisonment. His chauffeur had been nailed as he tried to get on I-5 back to California; his plates were a dead giveaway. He was convicted as an accessory.

Nobody paid for the damage to my office.

San Diego County and the City, working with Mexican authorities, were closing in on the Marcos operation. As part of the plea-bargaining process, Marcos spilled names – clients. The name of Fred Deloitte came up, very prominently.

One night, Fred Deloitte left his office and took the elevator to the parking garage. He got into his Mercedes, put a pistol into his mouth and pulled the trigger.

When my sons came to visit during a school holiday, fifteen year-old Jason asked, "Dad, do you remember when I asked you about the good guys and the bad guys, a long time ago? You said that the good guys win only when they are stronger, faster and smarter than the bad guys! Do you remember that?" And we did a big and long, long hug.

CHAPTER TWENTY-FIVE ———————

ONE EVENING, MISSY AND I talked about the future.

Missy would study law, after graduation from WWU. This was firm. She had, from the age of twelve, witnessed and endured an unspeakable injustice. This was to form her career. There was so much to do. We knew her debating skills; the California state championship was but frosting on the cake of an impeccable record. She would have her choice of law schools, we knew. We have the money. All you need is the grades, Missy.

"By the way, I haven't seen anything like a report card, or what do you call it?"

"Oh," she said, waving the idea away. "I have a 4.00 average. You can see it if you want." I was asking Mario Andretti if he had passed his driving test.

"I believe you. But can we put it on the refrigerator door?"

When she left for law school, I would leave Abe to manage the company and go with her. After her graduation, we would return to Whatcom County, where she would practice law. And start a family. This was our home. We would not leave Mt. Baker and the glaciers and the snow and the Nooksack River.

Missy was working part-time for Ray as a trainee paralegal. And she still found time to tutor foster children. "Hamlin, when they move to a foster home, or from one home to another, not only are their personal lives disrupted again, but they usually have to change schools, too. They lose continuity in their schoolwork; at the same time they lose their family, and their friends. So a tutor can help them to catch up, even provide some emotional support.

Hamlin, it's really sad. Sometimes these kids go to a new foster home with all their clothes and belongings in a plastic bag. There are good foster parents and bad foster parents, but the stipend from the state is almost nothing. They get $100 a year for clothing! Can you imagine? And there is no money for piano or ballet lessons, or sports uniforms, or camping trips, stuff like that." And Missy was looking distressed and teary, as though the cares of all the children in the world were in her lap. I had seen credit card slips for children's clothing and sports equipment, even a bicycle, once.

There were a few times when Abe had to beg off a late afternoon or evening assignment, and didn't want to say why, and I had let it go.

And one day I asked Missy if Abe was tutoring kids too.

"Oh, didn't he tell you?"

Then I found out that she had recruited Frieda, for Saturday tutoring.

And the lyrics of a Kris Kristofferson song came around in my mind; the story was some small kindnesses in a rough roadhouse cafe, with the refrain:

> "Ain't that just like a human;
> Here comes that rainbow again."

Missy, the recruiter. And the big hearts all around me. The rainbow, indeed.

We started taking kids to the cabin on weekends, two boys or two girls at a time. We took long hikes. And the looks of wonder on the faces of those children as they saw the magnificent beauty of the mountain and its glaciers, the forests and the river, were our reward beyond measure.

And then we started bringing four kids; the girls would sleep in the loft, and we put futons on the floor of the big room for the boys. And the kids had some family again, if only for a weekend, and maybe memories of a long- ago vacation before their parents went away. I guess that my favorite was Edward, who came from a foster home that presented no apparent hope for his future; his whole life centered on weekends here on the mountain and the river.

And Missy always insisted that they bring their homework, to work on for an hour each evening as we fixed dinner.

*   *   *

"Hamlin Cross, do you love me?" Missy was lying near me on our bed, looking at me as I read a Paul Theroux novel on a lazy afternoon. She had been puttering in our small garden for a while. She had just showered and toweled, and was in a short terry cloth bathrobe. She was up on her elbows, her chin cradled in her hands.

"You bet your sweet bippy I do!" I replied.

Pause. "And just what is a 'bippy'?"

Uh-oh. Hamlin the anachronism. I put down my book.

"You're a university student, and you don't know what a 'bippy' is? Check your Gray's Anatomy. It's the proper anatomical term for this!" I said as I reached over, lifted the hem of her robe, and bit the right cheek of her bippy. She gave a happy little scream.

"And do you find my bippy sweet?"

"Is one part of a gumdrop less sweet than the rest?"

Theroux was tossed aside. And there was no more talk of bippies or anything else for about an hour.

*   *   *

One evening as we sipped our coffee after dinner, Missy jumped up. "I'm going to show you something!"

She took down the silver picture frame from the mantle, and opened the back. Under the photo of the three friends was another print, of Missy and me in the hut.

"That's how I hid it from my Mom!"

I looked at Missy with wonder.

"Hamlin, I never forgot you!"

*   *   *

One evening, she said, "Hamlin, I have to tell you something really silly. Promise you won't laugh? When I heard you singing outside the hut, when you scrubbed yourself, I didn't know what you were singing. But I never forgot the melody. And one day, years later, I think it was in a music appreciation class or something, when I heard the singing, and I had to hide my eyes, because I remembered that time when you and I were together, and that was the only song that could connect us. After I was twelve, I understood clearly what had happened in those four days and I remember that you never made a big deal out of it, as though you and I were together naturally, there was nothing else to do but to get off the mountain together. But I heard at school on that day the lady singing opposite the male singer - and my heart almost burst, wishing I could be that girl singing along with you! It was the Drinking Song from *La*

Traviata. I always knew that I wanted to find you -- long before I found out what they did to you -- but I wanted to sing that song with you!!"

One night in bed, I asked Missy the question she frequently asked me. "Sarah Cross, do you really love me?"

She jumped like a startled deer. Her eyes were wide with disbelief. Her mouth dropped. Missy touched my arm, and looked at me helplessly. The girl who had slain dragons and giants with her words, had no more words to use.

"Hamlin…don't you know......" And the tears started.

I was sorry that I had done this. I knew that her regular questioning of my love for her was really a game, dining table and pillow talk, done for fun. But this was serious; she had been impaled by my question.

"I know you do, Missy. I know you love me as much as I love you."

As we enveloped in a rush of faces, arms and legs, we were melded into one. And we reaffirmed our mutual love for a long, long time.

*　　　　*　　　　*

One day, Missy asked "Can we go to Lee's hut sometime?"

"Sure. It's still there, and a bit improved. He told me that the stove is operating, and he's got more food, and a good supply of kerosene and wood. And a chemical toilet out back. It's like before but better. He has people who go up in a snowmobile to drop supplies, so no one has to carry them as before. We can do it in a day trip, but it will be all day. And we'll have to start early."

She stared at me. Is this guy really dense? "Hamlin, I want to sleep with you in that bed in Lee's hut again."

"Ok, but please don't lose your skis this time. I really can't carry you on my back again!"

So we did an overnight at Lee's hut. We had a commemorative dinner of canned vegetable beef soup and crackers, this time with an apple for dessert, and with a candle on the table. And we read Robert Frost again after dinner.

And if beds had memories, it would have recorded that this was the most exciting night, and maybe the noisiest, of its history.

The next morning, Missy said, "Hamlin, I think that this bed is where I first learned about love! Even if not about sex! Maybe we could put a plaque on the headboard, if it had one!"

"Well, why don't we bring a headboard next time, and bolt it on the end. Then we will put a brass plaque on it."

"But what will it say?"

"How about the dates, and 'Two people who really loved each other slept here and didn't do it'?"

"Don't put that on the plaque. Anyway, we made up for it this time!"

"We did," I groaned. "Will you carry me on your back on the way down?"

*   *   *

One night, as we crossed between sleep and dim wakefulness, Missy peered into my face and asked, "Hamlin, do you really love me?" It was a challenge to give new and clever answers each time, and often my imagination was taxed, and that night, I was just tired and couldn't think. I answered. For once, I wanted to skip the jokes and give a simple, direct and true answer.

"Missy, do you understand that no one in the history of the world has ever loved anyone as much as I love you?"

Missy was on her elbows in bed, looking at my face in the dim light as I said this. She didn't move for a while. Then she turned off the lamp, settled down, and nestled next to me in our usual starting sleeping position, with my arms around her. And I felt her crying a little bit, and I squeezed her harder in a hug powered by a love that I knew would never, ever stop, no matter how many times this goofy earth spins around that sun.

CHAPTER TWENTY-SIX ──────

THE OLD MAN LAY IN his bed in the half-darkened room, facing the ceiling, alone with his memories. The medication had been so strong recently, that his thoughts were really only brief recollections fading into dreams, in and out of wakefulness and sleep. It was hard to hold old, pleasant thoughts for more than a moment, and he tried to cling to each before it went away. The boys were always there – the ball games and camping trips, the dining table antics, the evening story and poems before bed.

And always, the greatest moment of his life – this was always clear. He sat alone in black tie with half the world watching, and hearing ... "and the award for the Best Original Screenplay is.................Hamlin Sullivan for *Bong Trees in Bellingham!*"

And he remembered the screaming roar, the standing ovation as he rose and stumbled, nearly blinded by tears, to the stage...

And then his boys again. They were going to visit soon...

The pain was getting worse. He hadn't been on his feet for two weeks, when he had put in a brief appearance at the annual Bellingham Bong Tree Festival. Every year before, he had been Grand Marshall of the parade. It was a lot of commercial hype, he accepted, but it was good for tourism and business, so good for the city. And it was his city.

He knew that this was his last Festival. The cancer had almost completed its work. "Mr. Sullivan," a nurse said softly, "it's time for your medication." After she left, there was only quiet.

As he drifted in and out of sleep and pain, the door opened, with an unaccustomed brilliance behind it. He saw the figure of a young girl, backlit with radiance as she crossed the room. It's not time for medication, he thought. And he saw that she had no nurse's cap nor uniform. A visitor? It wasn't visiting hours. But who?

As she neared his bed, he saw that the girl was wearing a red and blue ski suit, with red curls spilling from a yellow cap. And as her face drew close to his, he saw clearly.

The girl slid one hand into his, covered it with her other, and kissed him gently on his cheek.

"Hamlin," she said. "I've come to take you home."

CHAPTER TWENTY-SEVEN ———————

"HAMLIN SULLIVAN, 73, PASSED AWAY peacefully at 10:30 p.m. yesterday, at St. Joseph's Hospital, after a six-month bout with cancer.

Mr. Sullivan, a noted screenwriter and novelist, was best known for his screenplay for the movie, *Bong Trees in Bellingham*, for which he won an Academy Award for Best Original Screenplay. He also won a National Book Award for the subsequent novel, based on the screenplay. He wrote two well-received sequel novels, part of the so-called "Missy Trilogy" which, like the original, held prominent places on the New York Times Bestseller list. He also wrote a well-acclaimed series of short stories, one of which, "The Marching Band", was the basis for a popular movie.

Mr. Sullivan was a long-time Bellingham resident. He received a BA in Electrical Engineering from the University of Texas, San Antonio, and an MA in Asian Studies from International Christian University in Tokyo, Japan. He was active in local charitable activities, notably organizations supporting disadvantaged children. He was a member of the Pacific Northwest Writers' Conference, and was frequently on the national lecture circuit, chiefly for charitable fundraising activities. Mr. Sullivan was an Adjunct Professor of Literature at Western Washington University, and a frequent guest lecturer at the University of Washington.

Mr. Sullivan never married. He is survived by a brother, Frederic, of Naples, Florida; a sister, Carmela, of Algarve, Portugal; and several nieces and a nephew.

There will be a ceremony at the Bellingham Methodist Church at 10:00

a.m. on Friday. Mr. Sullivan's ashes are to be scattered in an undisclosed location in the Mt. Baker area, in accordance with his wishes. The family asks that, in lieu of flowers, a donation be made to Blue Skies for Children, 13 Prospect Street, Bellingham WA 98228."

The End